THE TRUTH
AND NOTHING BUT
THE TRUTH

"Is Fez really okay?" Callie asked.

"Um—"

"Carole, tell me," Callie said.

"He's changed, Callie. There's no spark in his eyes, no alert flick of his ears. He's weak; he's tired. He has trouble standing and even more walking. He came down out of the van like he knew that the quicker he did it, the quicker he could lie down again. That's not the same horse that took us forty-five minutes to get off the van when he first arrived at Pine Hollow. He's not okay. Definitely not okay. What I don't know—what nobody knows—is if that's going to change."

"Thank you for not sugarcoating. I get an awful lot of that from my family, and it's nice to hear something that's clearly the unvarnished truth—even if I don't like it much."

"I'm not very good at sugarcoating," said Carole. "I never have been."

"And that's why we're going to get along," said Callie.

PINE HOLLOW™

THE TRAIL HOME

BY BONNIE BRYANT

BANTAM BOOKS
NEW YORK • TORONTO • LONDON • SYDNEY • AUCKLAND

RL 5.0, ages 12 and up

THE TRAIL HOME

A Bantam Book / October 1998

"Pine Hollow" is a trademark of Bonnie Bryant Hiller.

ISBN 0-553-49243-8

Published simultaneously in the United States and Canada

Bantam Books are published by Bantam Books, a division of Bantam
Doubleday Dell Publishing Group, Inc. Its trademark, consisting of the
words "Bantam Books" and the portrayal of a rooster, is Registered in
U.S. Patent and Trademark Office and in other countries. Marca
Registrada. Bantam Books, 1540 Broadway, New York, New York
10036.

PRINTED IN THE UNITED STATES OF AMERICA

OPM   0 9 8 7 6 5 4 3 2 1

For my boys, Emmons and Andy

ONE

Nothing had been the same since the accident. Stevie Lake only had to close her eyes to bring back every terrifying detail, from the dark blur of the horse that raced in front of her car to the ceaseless flapping of the windshield wipers to the utter silence that told her and her friend Carole that something was wrong—really wrong—with Callie.

Callie had been in the backseat. The old car didn't have shoulder belts back there. Callie had been tossed around like a rag doll as the car tumbled. She was unconscious, concussed, and seriously hurt. They had known that much when the ambulance had taken her away.

Carole and Stevie had been merely bumped, bruised, and cut. Stevie had broken ribs as well. But they were okay. They slept at home that night in their own beds, while Callie stayed in the hospital, watched carefully by the doctors and her family, recovering first from the acci-

1

dent and then from the emergency surgery that had relieved the pressure on her brain.

The doctors reassured everybody. They told Callie's father, Congressman Forester, that they were doing everything possible. They told her mother and her brother, Scott, that they were pretty sure Callie would be all right. They told the reporters who waited impatiently outside the hospital for updates about the congressman's daughter that she was resting comfortably.

Nothing anybody said could reassure Stevie. She'd been behind the wheel of the car. She was the one who had swerved to avoid the terrified horse. She was the one who had put Callie in the hospital, who had nearly killed her, and who was now responsible for the injuries that remained—and might remain forever. Callie's bones had knit, her cuts had healed, her bruises faded, but there was something else. One of the doctors called it residual brain damage.

Residual. That meant left over. There was no telling how long it would be left over or if it would be left over forever. The realization that it might be forever left a dull, persistent ache in Stevie's heart. It didn't matter how many people told her she couldn't have prevented the accident; she was the one who had been driving. Callie's life had been in her hands, and her

2

hands alone. Something had gone wrong, and Callie was paying for it. That was *residual*.

Callie's doctor thought horseback riding would be good for her. It would strengthen her muscles, help her balance, and give her confidence. The doctor called it therapeutic riding. It was an ironically logical solution, making everything seem simple and neat: the rider healing herself through riding. But the fact was that nothing was simple; everything was complicated. Stevie was overwhelmed by all the complications—most of them caused by her.

"Look at that," Carole said, pointing down to the ring, where Callie was having her first therapeutic riding session.

Stevie was acutely aware of everything that was going on below them. She and Carole were sitting in a shady spot on a hillside overlooking the schooling ring, where Callie was the lone rider amid a large group of instructors, supporters, and well-wishers.

"It's as if she's on a horse for the first time," Stevie said. "And I bet it feels that way to her, too."

"I bet," Carole agreed.

Down in the ring, Callie looked around nervously. She was in the saddle—a place she'd spent countless hours over many, many years—but it didn't feel the way it had before. Ever since the accident, her right side had refused to be what it had been. She could move everything, wave her fingers, wiggle her toes, but none of it felt quite right. It was as if there was a delay in getting the instructions from her mind to her limbs. And they weren't strong. She had trouble raising her right arm and moving it forward. Her leg seemed stiff, like an unfamiliar appendage. Was it hers, really? It certainly wasn't the same leg she'd always thought she'd had. When it moved, it kind of jerked. She was unsure whether it would hold her, move her forward, help her turn, stand up, sit down, or lie down. And when she got tired it got worse.

Now, here she was, sitting in the saddle of this sweet-natured horse named PC, and even just standing there, Callie was acutely aware that the horse was doing a lot more work than she was.

"Good job!" the physical therapist said.

"I haven't done anything," Callie told her.

"That means you haven't done anything wrong yet," Emily Williams said wryly.

Callie smiled. Emily had a way of finding high points in a flat landscape.

Emily was Callie's age, and it was her horse Callie was riding. Emily had years of experience with therapeutic riding because she'd been born with cerebral palsy. Walking on her own two

4

feet, Emily was disabled. She needed her crutches, and if she got overtired, she had to use her hated wheelchair. She'd been riding for years, and she loved every minute she spent with PC, because when she was in the saddle, she was everybody's equal. She could walk, trot, and canter just as well as anybody else. Some people thought she loved riding because it helped her forget that she was disabled. That wasn't quite right, though, because she accepted her disability as part of herself; it wasn't something that ever went away. What she loved about riding was that *other* people forgot she was disabled. That was a gift she treasured. Now she wanted Callie to learn about it, too. She wouldn't learn today, not on her first day in the saddle, but soon, Emily was sure.

"Okay now, PC," Emily said. "Let's make Callie do some work." She passed the lead line to Ben Marlow, a stable hand, and clucked her tongue. Obediently PC began walking.

It took Callie a second to adjust to the pace— not that it was fast. She was moving, and for the first time since her accident, she was moving smoothly. There was no jerk or hesitation in PC's step. She sighed to herself.

"Not too fast there, Ben," Scott Forester interjected.

"It's just a walk!" Callie chided her brother.

"Well, it looks like a fast walk to me," Scott said.

"Slow down, boy," Emily said as if she meant it, but neither Ben nor the horse slowed down a bit.

Callie was so focused on the work she was doing—and there was no doubt that it *was* work—that she was almost unaware of her brother's concern. Scott wasn't the natural-born rider that his sister was. He was a natural-born talker—star of every debate team he'd ever been on—and destined to be a politician like his father.

"She'll be fine as long as she isn't distracted," Ben said, speaking for the first time as he continued to lead PC across the ring. Ben had all the patience in the world for horses. He didn't have much tolerance for people, though, and that seemed to include Scott in particular.

Scott merely glared at him, but he did stop fretting out loud. He stepped back and stood by his parents. His father slung an arm over his shoulder.

Up on the hillside, Carole and Stevie could see it all, and although they couldn't hear, they knew what was going on.

"I don't think Scott is ever going to speak to me again," Stevie said.

"Oh, he'll get over it," said Carole.

"He told me I should have just hit the horse and been done with it. That was what he said, 'and been done with it.' "

"If he knew anything about horses or driving, he would know that if a car hits a horse, there aren't any winners. You swerved, and it probably saved all of our lives. Even the police investigation said so."

"I wonder," Stevie said.

"Don't. It's true," said Carole. "There's no point in wondering about it."

"No, I don't mean that. I mean, I wonder how much I saved," Stevie said. "Look at Callie."

"She's going to be fine," said Carole.

"Maybe. And then there's Fez."

Fez was the horse Stevie had swerved to avoid hitting. She'd hit him anyway, and the impact had sent the car tumbling down the hillside. The horse had been left on the road, badly hurt.

If he hadn't been so valuable, he would have been put down right away. He'd broken a leg that wasn't going to heal easily, if at all. As part of his recovery, he'd spent some time suspended in a tank of water that kept his weight off the leg. Most owners couldn't afford to give their horses the kind of treatment Fez had received, but the Foresters had insisted that the vet do everything possible to save him.

"Maybe Fez'll make it; maybe he won't," Carole said.

"You sound like you almost don't care," said Stevie. "An odd thought for somebody who's never met a horse she didn't like."

Carole smiled. "Fez might possibly be the exception to that," she said, shaking her head. Fez was a top-level endurance horse, and some of the qualities that made him a champion in that sport made him difficult to love, from Carole's point of view. Endurance riding demanded enormous spirit, heart, and determination from both horse and rider. In the case of Fez, that also seemed to translate into stubbornness. Carole had been exercising him and found herself at odds with the animal almost every time she rode him. He'd been a challenge she hadn't met easily. And then she'd seen Callie ride him and it had been as if he were a different animal. Callie knew exactly how much room to give him to let him strut his stuff. He was fiery, to be sure, but Callie managed him by letting him at least think he was in charge. It was a formidable partnership.

Another part of Fez's spirit came from his total awareness of what was going on around him. He was highly sensitive and reacted to everything, which meant he spooked easily. He'd been out in the paddock when the freak thunderstorm struck, and the lightning had terrified him into jumping a four-and-a-half-foot fence onto the road, straight into the path of Stevie's car.

"But just because I didn't like riding Fez doesn't mean I don't care about him," Carole said.

"Oh, I know that. A day hasn't gone by that you haven't either stopped by the clinic or called to find out how he was doing."

"And every time I stopped by, you were there, too," Carole reminded her.

"A pair of softies, that's what we are," said Stevie. "Besides, it was a way to avoid the journalists who wanted to talk to me all the time. At the hospital, at home, every time I turned around, there they were. Somehow or other they never located the clinic." Right after the accident, Stevie had been flooded with requests for interviews. Reporters wanted to talk to the driver of the car that had so seriously hurt "the congressman's daughter." It hadn't helped Stevie's own recovery at all.

Stevie and Carole watched the rest of the lesson in silence, enjoying the interaction between horse and rider. It didn't seem odd to either of them that in this instance the horse was doing more of the instructing than the rider.

The two girls, along with their friend Lisa

Atwood, who was spending the summer in California, had ridden together for a long time. Riding was something they always enjoyed, even when it was work, and for each of them there had been times when the very act of riding was itself an act of healing.

Carole glanced at Stevie, who was sitting still, intently watching Callie and Emily, and watching the people who were watching Callie and Emily. Carole hoped Callie's healing would mark the beginning of Stevie's healing. Stevie might be able to fool some people about how well she had recovered from the trauma of the accident and the crush of journalists, but she couldn't fool Carole. Carole knew that the smile on Stevie's face masked enormous doubt and pain in her heart. Stevie, after all, had been the one behind the wheel, and now nothing was the same.

TWO

In the schooling ring below, Carole saw that the session was coming to an end. Ben brought PC to a halt at the mounting block, where the therapist and Callie's father were waiting to help Callie dismount.

"C'mon," Carole said, standing up. "Let's go give a hand with the tack and grooming. PC could use some help."

Stevie looked doubtful. "Don't you think there are enough people to help already?"

Of course there were. There were a half dozen people watching this first session, but Carole didn't think that was the point. "They're all there to look after Callie. You and I should take care of PC."

"Okay," Stevie agreed, somewhat reluctantly. Not for a minute did Carole think that Stevie's hesitation had anything to do with PC or the idea of looking after a horse. It had nothing to do with horses and everything to do with people. Since Stevie still blamed herself for what had happened, Carole knew she was certain others did, too. "Others" included Callie's parents and brother. Stevie wasn't eager to face them again. Carole wasn't going to be deterred. She gave Stevie a hand and pulled her to her feet.

"Last one down there is a . . ."

"Chicken?" Stevie supplied.

Carole didn't respond, just hurried down the hillside. Stevie followed more slowly.

They arrived at the dismounting area to find that Callie was still receiving congratulations on her session.

"You did really well," the therapist was saying.

"A good start," said Emily.

"You must be very tired," said her mother.

"Would you like me to carry you?" her father asked.

Carole winced for Callie. It had to be extremely annoying to have all those well-wishers standing around telling her how she felt.

As she watched the group crowding around Callie, Carole thought back to their first meeting. The two hadn't hit it off. Carole had been put off by what she regarded as Callie's arrogance and need for special treatment. Gradually she'd realized that Callie wasn't arrogant, merely shy and uncomfortable in a new situation. Unfortunately, Carole had let her first impression affect the way she behaved toward the new girl. Then, before she could apologize and suggest that they start fresh, the accident had happened. Suddenly those minor differences didn't seem important anymore. Now, as Callie began her journey to recovery, Carole was determined that they would both start over as friends.

For now, Carole didn't see any point in adding to the confusion. She just smiled at Callie and took the horse's lead rope to walk him back to his stall. Stevie followed.

"Here, dear, I'll get your crutches," said Mrs. Forester.

"I can carry her," Congressman Forester said.

Carole and Stevie were aware of a lot of chatter as they did the routine but enjoyable work that was part of riding. That meant untacking, grooming, watering, and feeding the sweet horse that had just exerted so much effort for their friend. They worked in silence, which was more than could be said about the others who were there.

The therapist wanted to talk with Emily about future sessions, since she couldn't be there every time. They had worked out a plan that would help Callie rebuild strength in her muscles and, with some luck and skill, overcome the residual brain damage from the accident.

Callie's parents talked intently with Max Regnery, the owner of Pine Hollow. Max had been instructing a class during the beginning of the session, but once the class was over, he had joined the well-wishers. They stood outside PC's stall, so Carole and Stevie could hear that they were discussing Fez. The injured horse would be returning to Pine Hollow soon, released from the clinic.

"We're going to work with our vet—you've met Judy Barker, haven't you? Well, she's the best. And we'll do whatever we can," Max said.

Carole listened, but she didn't know what the Foresters were saying until Max answered them.

"No," he said. "It's not a matter of money. He'll get whatever care he needs. And whatever care seems best."

Carole and Stevie exchanged glances. "As if Max, or anyone here, could possibly ignore the needs of any horse!" Stevie whispered, giving PC a final brush and pat.

Pine Hollow was a long-established stable with a lot of traditions. One of the strongest ones was that everybody there worked. When the girls were younger, they had thought that the primary reason for that was to keep costs down, and it certainly did that. When riders pitched in, it meant that the place needed fewer paid staff members, and that made riding accessible to more people.

But it had taken a while for the girls to understand that there was a lot more to it. By helping, by looking after their own horses and often pitching in to help with other people's, they'd learned that riding didn't start when you got into the saddle and end when you dismounted. Riding was taking responsibility for your horse as well as riding it. That resulted in another of Pine Hollow's traditions: turning out well-trained, successful horsemen and horsewomen. Pine Hollow's "graduates" had earned lots of ribbons at prestigious horse shows, and some had gone on to distinguished careers in different aspects of riding, horse care, and stable management. Carole intended to be among them.

"I'll get his water bucket," Carole said.

Stevie went to get a fresh tick of hay. When she returned, she found that almost everybody was at PC's stall. It looked like a tableau, with the players surrounding the featured characters. Callie was rubbing PC's nose while the gentle horse chomped on a carrot she'd given him. Scott stood nearby, looking tense, as if the act of petting the horse could endanger his sister. The therapist looked proud, as if she'd invented therapeutic riding. Emily, clearly pleased that she'd been able to help, was holding on to PC's halter with what looked like great pride of ownership. Ben was there, too, but he stood back, silent as usual.

Carrying PC's bucket, Carole made her entrance into the scene. The tableau broke apart, letting her into the stall.

"Good start," she said to Callie while she hooked the bucket on the wall.

"I guess it was," Callie said. She nodded, pleased, because what Carole had said was true. It was good, and it was a start, but it was only a start . . . but it *was* good.

"Were you afraid?" Carole asked her.

Scott recoiled at the question. He obviously didn't like the idea that someone would challenge his sister's courage. He started to protest, but Callie cut him off.

"You bet," she said. "But it worked out okay. I like riding again, and this feels right."

"Aren't you tired and ready to go home?" Scott asked.

"Not quite," said Callie. "As long as everybody's here, you can save me a lot of work—"

"Anything we can do . . . ," Carole said quickly.

"Not that kind of work," said Callie. "Like writing out invitations kind of work. Mom and Dad are planning a party for this weekend—on

Saturday. You're all invited." She looked around at everyone. Ben looked away, embarrassed.

Callie saw that. "You, too, Ben, of course," she said. "Definitely, all of you. It's sort of a welcome-home party for me. In the backyard, cookout, swimming pool—the whole deal. Dad says he won't even mind if we play music he doesn't know how to dance to. It's time we had some fun, don't you think?"

"Great idea," Carole said.

"Can you come, Emily?" Callie said.

"Sure. I wouldn't miss it."

"Stevie?"

Stevie glanced at Scott. He didn't look at her. It was probably just as well. If he had looked at her, it would have been a glare and Stevie would have chickened out. This party was for Callie, not Scott. "Of course I'll be there," she said.

"You can bring Phil, too."

"Okay, I'll see if he can come," Stevie said, hoping very much that he would be able to. Phil, her boyfriend, would provide a good distraction from Scott's moody glares.

"Come on, honey. Time to go home now," Congressman Forester said, joining the teenagers in the stable. He offered his arm to his daughter. Callie looked at it briefly and then took it. She was tired. It was clear to everyone that she was grateful for the support.

The crowd dispersed. Emily gave PC a final pat and followed Callie to the car, chatting with Scott as they went. Carole took PC's saddle to the tack room, and Ben picked up a pitchfork and began mucking out a stall down the aisle.

Stevie stood and watched Callie. She cringed with each awkward step the girl took. It was her fault. All of it was her fault.

THREE

After Callie's first session, Carole wasn't in any hurry to leave Pine Hollow. She packed a tired Emily off to her own home, telling her she'd finish looking after PC. Stevie had disappeared, and Carole wasn't surprised. The day had been hard on her.

Carole wondered how she'd feel if she'd been the one behind the wheel. It wouldn't matter how many times she was told it wasn't her fault: she wouldn't be any more ready to believe it than Stevie was. It was one thing to consider the matter abstractly: *You did everything right. It wasn't your fault. Nobody would have done anything different. It could have been so much worse.* It was another thing to watch Callie struggle with each step.

When Carole returned from the tack room, PC was waiting for her expectantly. Horses seemed to understand that a nice grooming and a rubdown were the payoff they got for a job well done. PC was smart enough to know that he'd done a good job.

Carole scratched him affectionately on the cheek and patted his neck. It only took a few minutes to finish grooming him and give him his fresh hay and another handful of carrots. She gave him one last pat for good-bye and then stepped out of his stall, sliding the bolt into place behind her.

She could hear someone working in a stall down the aisle. Curious, Carole followed the sound of hay being pitched expertly. By the sound of the third forkful, she knew it was Ben. It was funny how someone who said so little with words could say so much through his work.

Right then Carole wasn't feeling terribly social herself, but she decided to see what Ben was up to and give him a hand. She picked a shovel off the rack and went back down the aisle.

Ben looked up when she appeared. If she hadn't known him better, she might have thought he almost smiled when he saw her.

"Thought you could use a hand," she said.

He answered with something that was more a grunt than a word. She took it as a thank-you and used her shovel to help clean the stall floor. When the wheelbarrow was full, she rolled it out to the manure pile and returned, picking up a fresh load of straw on the way. Together they spread the sweet grass on the floor of the stall— a stall that had been empty since the accident. That was when Carole looked at the nameplate on the stall door. The brass was still shiny and new, the name clear and clean: FEZ.

"He's coming back today?" Carole asked.

"Needs a clean stall," said Ben.

"Is he—?"

"Judy and Max talked. She says she's done everything she can. It's time for him to come home."

"Today?" Carole asked, repeating the question Ben hadn't answered.

"Looks that way," he said. He glanced at his watch, offering no further information on the subject. Ben could be pretty infuriating—if you took that sort of thing personally. It wouldn't have occurred to Carole to give so little information. Then she realized that, from Ben's point of view, he wasn't holding back information as much as speculation. He really wouldn't know if Judy was actually going to bring the horse by that afternoon or if she might be delayed by an emergency with another of her patients and put it off until the next day. Carole sighed. Fez would be there when Judy brought him, no matter when that was.

"Well, the place looks spick-and-span for our

returning guest. I'll go update the charts in his notebook so the office will be as ready for his arrival as the stall is."

Each of Pine Hollow's horses and residents had a notebook in which all the caretakers, instructors, owners, and various professionals, including the vet and the farrier, could make notations. In some ways it was like a patient's chart in a hospital. Most of the entries were pretty routine, noting feed blends, farrier appointments, and veterinary matters like immunizations and tests. Fez's chart was mostly empty, since he'd only been at Pine Hollow a short while before the accident. Nevertheless, Carole needed to make notations for the records about his recovery since the accident, and she would have to put in whatever information and recommendations Judy had for Fez's recuperative care.

Carole went to the desk that was partly hers because she was Pine Hollow's morning stable manager for the summer, and took out his chart. She reread the details of the accident and described the terrible bolt of lightning and violent clap of thunder that had spooked Fez into jumping the high fence and racing directly in front of Stevie's car. In the future, if there was a future, anyone reading his record would know that Fez was deathly afraid of thunder and lightning.

Carole shifted the notebook to write on it better. She found that it was resting on a pile of papers she hadn't noticed when she'd first sat down. It wasn't unusual for a pile of papers to appear on the desk suddenly, since Max sometimes left things for her attention. In fact, the office often seemed a little disorganized, much like the tack room that abutted it. It could have been described as disorganized organization. It looked messy, but those who knew the system could find anything.

Carole lifted the notebook to find out what the papers were all about.

They were a form of some kind. At the top of the first sheet was a logo, then the word *application,* followed by some handwritten information.

"That's mine," Ben said, yanking the papers out of Carole's hand before her eyes could even focus on the contents.

"Uh, sorry," she said automatically. "I thought Max might have left something for me—"

"It's okay, but they're mine," he said, cutting her off. He folded the pages quickly and stuffed them into his back pocket. "I'm going for a bucket of Fez's feed. He'll be hungry when he gets here." Before Carole could say another word of apology—or any word at all—he was back out the door, headed for the grain shed.

Once again Ben had successfully avoided any kind of informative conversation, apparently deferring to the needs of a horse.

Carole glanced down at the desk before replacing the notebook. The envelope for Ben's papers was still there, addressed to him. It had the same logo the application had. It was from the local Horsemen's Association, and under the address was handwritten *Scholarship Committee*.

The pieces of the puzzle slid into place. Ben had graduated from high school a year before. Carole could still remember his embarrassed smile when the Pony Club had given him a card signed by all the members, Carole, Lisa, and Stevie included. Max had told him to take a day off work for graduation, but he'd only been gone for the morning, returning that afternoon in his usual sensible work clothes but with a fresh haircut—no doubt obligatory. Nothing had been said about the graduation itself, and it seemed to mean little to Ben, other than that he could work longer hours at Pine Hollow.

Now, apparently, Ben was applying for the Horsemen's Association's scholarship, which meant he intended to go on to college. There were a couple of colleges in the area that offered good equine studies programs. Carole knew about them because she intended to apply to one or more of them in another year herself. She'd also known about the scholarship from the Horsemen's Association. What she hadn't known was that Ben was applying now.

That was great news. And of course it made a lot of sense. Ben didn't talk much, but he was one of the most naturally gifted horsemen she'd ever known. He'd never have trouble getting work with horses, but a college degree, especially one in equine studies, would make a big difference in the kind of work he'd get.

Since Ben had arrived at Pine Hollow, Carole had seen a lot of him. She'd watched him calm upset horses, train fidgety ones, and tend sick ones. He'd fed them, groomed them, dosed them, exercised them, taught them. He seemed to speak to them in their own language, establishing a primal relationship with them. It was only people Ben couldn't talk to.

And now he wanted to go to college. Carole felt a small glow. She knew a secret, and it was a good one. Ben deserved this. He deserved to go to college, and he deserved all the help that was available. He deserved scholarships and recognition. He deserved everything she and her friends could do for him.

While these thoughts still whirled in her head, Ben returned to the office.

"It's ready," he said.

"Good. Listen, Ben, I really wasn't snooping, but I want to say how happy I am that you're applying for the scholarship. I didn't know you were thinking about college . . ."

He didn't say anything, but the look he gave her made her stop talking. Carole blushed. She hadn't said what she'd wanted to say. It made it sound as if Ben were somehow different from other people—not the kind of person who should think about college. That wasn't what she meant at all, but Ben's look told her that that was what he'd heard.

"Well, good luck," she said, backing off.

"It's not really about luck," he said, once again turning aside her good wishes.

Carole swallowed any further words that came into her head. There was no point. Ben would turn anything she said into what he expected to hear. That wasn't fair, but she couldn't do anything about it. He thought of himself as a second-class citizen, but she didn't, and she didn't want to be tarred with that brush.

"Right," she said.

At that awkward moment, they both heard a

van coming up the drive to the stable. It had to be Judy Barker with Fez.

"I think our patient has come home from the hospital," Carole said.

"I hope he's easier to get off the van this time," Ben said.

Carole laughed. When Fez had first arrived at Pine Hollow, it had taken the two of them, a blindfold, ten carrots, and forty-five minutes to coax the reluctant traveler off the van and into his stall.

This time it was a very different story. Fez was a changed animal. He was submissive and meek. His head hung low with fatigue; his ears, once alert and flicking in every direction, now nearly flopped. He'd lived through a terrible ordeal and had more hard times to go.

"I don't know," Judy said, shaking her head as she led him down the gentle slope of the ramp. "I've got his leg in a splint. He can stand on it and walk a little. He'll spend most of his time lying down, but he loses muscle tone every time he doesn't use the leg, and it seems to be getting harder, rather than easier, for him to stand. I hate to say it, but I just don't know if this boy is going to make it. He doesn't need medicine now as much as he needs care. He needs exercise *and* rest—in careful proportions. Ben, Max said you have some ideas."

"I do," he said.

Carole smiled to herself. Almost anybody else in the world would have then given some idea of what the ideas were, but not Ben. Well, both Carole and Judy knew that whatever they were, they would be good ones, and if he had any questions, he'd ask. Ben would never, ever, under any circumstances, do anything that would hurt a horse.

Ben took the lead rope from Judy and, speaking gentle words into one of Fez's flopped ears, led him back to his stall. Except for his markings, it was almost impossible to recognize the horse. All the spark, all the fire, all the character that had made him both difficult and great were gone. Carole bit her lip, holding back the almost overwhelming emotion she felt watching the broken horse nearly stumble back to his home.

"We can take care of the paperwork," Carole said, inviting Judy into the office.

Judy sat down across the desk from Carole and handed her the medical records. She also gave her medicines that Ben and Max could administer to Fez and carefully described how they should be used. Carole took notes and stored the medicines in the small refrigerator near her desk. She closed the notebook, shelved it, and invited Judy to take a final look at her patient.

Walking along the hallway at Pine Hollow with Judy was always an experience. The vet never missed a chance to check on all her patients.

"I see Barq's been eating better," she said, rubbing the Arabian's nose and admiring the horse's recently more rounded belly. "And look, the scarring is almost all gone on Penny's flank. What's the matter with Nickel?"

"Nothing, as far as I know," Carole said, suddenly alert to a possible problem.

"He looks tired," said Judy.

"Oh, right, tired. Of course he is," said Carole. "The youngest kids were working on gait changes in class today. Poor old Nickel went from a walk to a trot to a canter about four hundred times. I'll see to it that he gets an apple tonight and a little molasses in his feed tomorrow."

"He'll thank me for that!" Judy said. "Hi, Starlight!" She patted his nose. "Oh, Belle, don't be jealous." She patted Belle's nose, too. "PC? How's it going?"

"It was his big day today," Carole said.

"Right. Callie was on him, wasn't she? How'd it go?"

"She was as tired as Nickel."

"I'll bet. And how did it go for Stevie?"

"Tough," said Carole.

"It would be," said Judy. "Now, Fez, are you glad to be home?" she asked, stopping outside his stall.

The horse lifted his eyes to take a look at his doctor. Ben stood by him, still murmuring gently, reassuringly. When he'd finished saying whatever he was telling the horse, he turned to Judy.

"We'll do fine together," he said.

"Tell me what you've got in mind for him," Judy said.

Ben unsnapped the horse's lead rope and moved to the stall's door. As he did so, Fez began a slow and pained descent to a lying position. Carole winced for him.

"Is it okay for him to do that?" she asked.

"Some," said Judy. "He shouldn't be putting too much weight on the leg for a while yet. The problem is that if he lies down too much, he'll lose all his muscle tone and he may never be able to get up again. He really needs to move as much as he can."

"That's what I want to work on," said Ben, latching the stall door behind him. "I was testing to see if he was well behaved enough to remain standing as long as I had him on the lead. It worked, and that means I should be able to walk him a little each day. Then, later, maybe more than a walk. I made a kind of chart." He

30

reached into his back pocket. "I'll show you." He pulled out the clutch of papers he'd taken off Carole's desk and unfolded them, turning to the third or fourth sheet.

He and Judy studied them together while Carole let the cobwebs clear out of her head. It only made sense that the Horsemen's Association scholarship application would require a competitive submission that would give the committee an idea of the skills the applicant already had. It had seemed odd, but now Carole understood why he'd pulled the application away from her so abruptly. It wasn't just his future that was on the line, it was his ego, too.

Ben had to show the papers to Judy. She'd have to oversee and approve his project. But he could keep his plan from Carole. That was all right by her, too. She didn't need to see exactly what he had in mind. The only thing she really needed to do was help him, though he wasn't likely to ask for help. She'd just have to give it to him—whether he realized he needed it or not.

Back when Carole, Lisa, and Stevie had first formed the group they called The Saddle Club, they had decided that, unlike a lot of other clubs, this one should have just two rules. The members had to be horse-crazy—which was the way they'd described themselves in those days—

and they had to be willing to do anything to help their friends. Every time they'd rolled up their sleeves to pitch in, they called it a Saddle Club project. But Lisa was a continent away. Stevie was working on her own project. This would be Carole's own personal Saddle Club project—whether or not Ben wanted it.

"This is good, Ben," Judy said when they'd finished going over the program. "You've planned for slow but steady progress, and you can be flexible if your patient either slows it down or speeds it up. The thing you don't know—can't know, really—is whether your patient will be able to cooperate at all. He's uncomfortable, even in pain a lot of the time. It's going to take a good deal of drive for him to move beyond the point he's already reached."

"He's going to be okay, isn't he?" Carole asked.

Judy shrugged. "I wish I could say yes, but I can't. It's a miracle he's alive right now. Almost any other horse with almost any other owner would have been euthanized at the scene of the accident. It was a bad break in a bad place. But the Foresters wanted me to do everything I could to save him. I always have mixed feelings about that. I mean, we're making progress every day in veterinary healing, and this gave me an opportunity to try new techniques and medicines, working with the clinic at the cutting edge. But the result . . ."

They all looked at Fez. He seemed more resigned than healed.

"Is he in constant pain?" Carole asked.

"No, I don't think so," said Judy. "If he were, there would be no question what I would recommend. He would have to be put down. I can't allow one of my patients to suffer constant pain. He gets sort of edgy sometimes, which I think means more discomfort, so I give him a sedative. Ben, you and Max can use it, too, if you sense he needs it.

"I'm worried about three things for him now, and everyone who looks after him will have to be aware of these. The first is that the bone has to complete its healing. It's not quite done, and it hasn't happened as fast as it ought to. That's why he's still got that splint on. Next, and Ben is focusing on this, Fez has got to build strength in all his muscles. Third is the possibility of a secondary infection. He's been through an enormous amount of work to get to the point he's reached, and it tends to lower an animal's resistance. He's okay now. He's stable, or I never would have brought him over here. And I don't like to have to say this, but if he doesn't—"

"Don't say it, Judy," Ben said, cutting her

off. "And don't worry. That's not going to happen. I've got a lot at stake here."

"I know, Ben. I know that. But you've got to remember that your success or failure as a trainer in this project is separate from the success or failure of the project."

"Failure?" he asked, saying the word as if he'd never heard it before. "No. We won't fail."

"Good luck," Judy said, offering him her hand. Ben reached to take it. She looked as if she wanted to say something else when the cell phone in her pocket started to ring. She answered the call, listened for a moment, shook her head, and said, "I'll be there." She hurried out of the stable before Ben had time to retract his hand or Carole had a chance to say goodbye.

FOUR

"I have to deliver an apple to Nickel, and then I'll come help you finish settling Fez in," Carole said.

"You don't have to help me," said Ben.

"No problem," Carole said. It was like Ben, frustratingly like Ben, to try to do everything by himself and to be too proud to ask for or even want help. However, it wasn't like Carole not to give a hand, so Ben would have to accept that part of her just the way she accepted the independent part of him.

It only took her a few minutes to fetch an apple for Nickel. There was always a supply of apples and carrots in the office refrigerator. She cut one apple into quarters, then cut another for Fez. What was good for Nickel would surely be good for Fez.

Nickel chomped his apple gratefully. By the next morning, he'd be rested and ready to go again. He was always a reliable pony for the young riders, who worked him hard.

Carole handed Ben the apple pieces, and he knelt by the resting horse. Fez lifted his head when he smelled the treat and nibbled rather than chomped at it. He seemed grateful for the apple, but not grateful enough to want to eat more than a quarter.

Ben stood up and wiped his hand on his jeans. He returned the leftover pieces to Carole.

They left Fez in his stall, latching it tightly more out of habit than need, since it seemed unlikely that Fez would be any threat to the stall lock. As they walked back down the stable aisle, Carole handed out the remaining pieces of fruit to the horses curious enough to wonder who was passing their stalls at this hour.

"I just have to lock up and then I'm on my way home. Can I give you a lift?" Carole said.

"Uh, no," said Ben. "I can walk."

"I know you can walk," she answered. "But I'd be happy to drive you."

"No, really. I'll walk."

For the first time, Carole realized she had no idea where Ben lived. He was such a quiet, private person, he never talked about his home. She'd never seen him leave or arrive. She hadn't known if he had a bicycle or was picked up and dropped off. For all she knew, he might have lived three towns away. Now she knew he walked. But that was all she knew, because it was all he let her know. If it wasn't easy to help him get home in the evening, it certainly wasn't going to be easy to help him look after Fez. She was determined, though, and she suspected that underneath it all, she could be just as stubborn as Ben Marlow.

"I think I'll stop by the Foresters' and see how Callie's doing. She'll want to hear about Fez, too. Want to come along?"

"No," he said. "I'm walking home."

Well, I guess we've established that, Carole thought.

"See you tomorrow, then," she said.

"Right."

He backed out of her office and into the shadows of the stable. Carole heard the sounds of his departure while she tidied her desk and took the keys out of the drawer. With a final good-night to the stable and the horses, she switched off the lights, locked the door behind her, and tucked the key into its more or less secret hiding place under the mat outside the office door.

She got into her car and started the engine. It was quite late, but the midsummer sky was just darkening past dusk. She switched on her headlights, backed up, turned, and pulled out of the driveway, turning right to go toward the Foresters'. It wasn't far, really just a few blocks away, in Stevie's neighborhood. Carole's own house was several miles away, on the edge of town.

As the car shifted up a gear, Carole saw Ben walking on the edge of the road. His hands were stuffed into the pockets of his jean jacket, his shoulders hunched forward and his head bowed into the darkness. He neither looked up nor acknowledged her wave as she drove past him.

The Forester house was cheerily lit when Carole pulled into the driveway. She didn't intend to stay long. She just wanted to see how Callie was doing and to report on Fez. Before she could reach the screen door, Scott was there to greet her.

"Hey, great. Callie? Guess who's here? It's Carole—from the stable. Come on in, Carole," he said warmly.

"Is it okay?" she asked.

"Of course it is," he said. "We were making plans for the barbecue, and your ideas will be welcome. In fact, you may be the very person we need, since there's a two-two tie on the issue of chicken versus ribs."

"You think you could lure me into taking sides against half of the family on such a critical issue?" Carole countered, following Scott through the house onto the back porch, where the Foresters were gathered.

"Well, I was going to try," he teased.

Carole hadn't been in the Foresters' house before. She liked it immediately. It reflected the same informal warmth that radiated from Scott and his father. Everything looked comfortable, everything looked nice, and it was welcoming, too. The back porch had a view of a sloping lawn that ended in a level area where there was a swimming pool. It was a perfect place for a barbecue.

Carole had barely greeted the family and sat down before Mrs. Forester left, then reappeared with a fresh bowl of popcorn.

"Can we ruin your appetite for dinner, Carole?" she asked with a warm smile.

"I wish you would," Carole said, taking a handful of popcorn. "It's my dad's night to cook."

The Foresters laughed, as Carole had known they would, and she cringed inside for a second at having taken a little dig at her father, who wasn't there to defend himself. She didn't mean anything by it. In fact, her father was a very good cook. They'd both learned a lot about cooking over the years since her mother had died, and they each did a respectable job of it, swapping nights of cooking and cleaning up.

Still, Carole was secretly pleased that she'd entertained the Foresters—even if the way she'd done it made her uncomfortable. Maybe it was time to get down to business.

"Judy brought Fez back to Pine Hollow after you'd left."

"How's he doing?" Callie asked.

"Okay," Carole said. "Pretty well, actually, considering what he's been through."

"Not wonderfully?"

"No," Carole said. "Not wonderfully." She could make light of her father's cooking, but she couldn't lie about a horse's condition. "He's healing, but he's in pain and his muscles are weak."

"I guess I know how that feels."

"I guess," Carole agreed. "Ben and I saw to it that he was comfortable. He was lying down and seemed okay when we left. We'll be watching him very closely. Ben has a plan for him. He's made up a regimen that will help him develop strength as soon as he can do any exercise at all."

"It's sort of like what Emily's worked out for me," said Callie.

"Sort of," Carole said. "And when the two of you ride together again—"

"*If,*" Callie said pointedly.

"Maybe it's an *if,* maybe it's a *when,*" said

Carole. "But it's more helpful to think of it in terms of *when*."

"For me?" Callie asked.

"For both of you," Congressman Forester said. "And the *when* can't come too soon. My dear, I was so proud of you today. It was wonderful to watch you ride. I know you're tired now and you may not have been as aware as I was of what was happening, but you were doing magnificently. I'm absolutely certain that there has already been some improvement—just as the doctor and the physical therapist said there would be—"

"After several *months*," Callie said, reminding her father of the facts of the matter.

"Perhaps, but you're already ahead of schedule, and as far as I'm concerned that's grounds for a celebration. Now, where were we on the chicken versus ribs debate?"

"It was ribs versus chicken," Scott countered. "Don't think you can jump in there and give chicken the upper hand simply by saying it first. Remember who the expert debater is here."

Mrs. Forester turned to Carole. "If a debate gets started there's simply no stopping these two," she said.

Carole smiled, but she wasn't really amused. It was almost like a show, put on for someone's benefit. Not her own, of course. They were

41

being funny for Callie, trying to make her feel better after what had truly been a trying day.

The debate progressed dramatically and humorously. Carole watched and listened for a while. This sort of banter was pleasant to be around, cheerful and cheering, but somehow a little empty. The carefree sparring of the two Foresters, father and son, stood in stark contrast to the recent conversations Carole had had with Ben. With Ben, there were things he didn't want to discuss, like the clutch of papers he kept jamming into his pocket. Carole didn't know what about those papers made him uncomfortable, but it was clear that he was not inviting any discussion of them. The Foresters also had things they didn't want to discuss—like the possibility that Callie's therapy might not be as successful as they all hoped it would. Instead of masking the subject with a frown, a grunt, or a turned head, Scott and his father seemed to be trying to drown it with jokes, gestures, and grandiose statements ("paying tribute to Maryland's finest chickens with your grandmother's piquant barbecue sauce, the recipe for which was carried over the Oregon Trail . . .").

Carole was lost in thought when the debate came to an abrupt halt.

"I think we should have both," Callie said.

"A call to compromise!" said her father.

"I bow to the brilliant suggestion by my younger sister," said Scott.

"I should have thought of that myself," said Mrs. Forester.

"I think I'd better get home now," Carole said.

"I'll see you to the door," Scott said.

"No, I will," Callie said, standing up unsteadily. She took a cane in one hand and accepted Carole's arm with the other. The two girls walked out together.

"Don't mind them," Callie said. "They're just trying to make me feel better."

"I know. I could tell," Carole said. "And I didn't mind them at all. I was just thinking about how much the two of them seem to enjoy arguing."

"They do. It can be annoying, but it can also be distracting. I don't really need to be distracted, but they seem to need to distract."

"Oh, of course," said Carole.

"Thanks for coming by. I'm glad to know that you and Ben are looking after Fez. Is he really okay?"

"Um—"

"Carole, tell me," Callie said.

"He's changed, Callie. There's no spark in his

eyes, no alert flick of his ears. He's weak; he's tired. He has trouble standing and even more walking. He came down out of the van like he knew that the quicker he did it, the quicker he could lie down again. That's not the same horse that took us forty-five minutes to get off the van when he first arrived at Pine Hollow. He's not okay. Definitely not okay. What I don't know—what nobody knows, really—is if that's going to change."

"Thank you for not sugarcoating. I get an awful lot of that from my family, and it's nice to hear something that's clearly the unvarnished truth—even if I don't like it much."

"I'm not very good at sugarcoating," said Carole. "I never have been."

"And that's why we're going to get along," said Callie.

Callie's mother joined them then. "What are you two talking about?" she asked.

"The barbecue, of course," said Carole. "I was just explaining to Callie that my father makes the finest barbecue in Virginia. It's old-fashioned, down-home Southern pork barbecue, and I didn't want to hurt anybody's feelings back there, but if I bring some to the party, nobody's going to eat the ribs or chicken."

"Then don't bring it," teased Mrs. Forester.

"I won't. But you'll have to come to our

house sometime and we'll settle this debate once and for all. Good night—and, um, Callie, it was good to see you back at Pine Hollow today."

"It was good to be there, Carole," Callie said. Carole knew she meant it.

FIVE

The following morning, Carole pulled into Emily's driveway. As usual, Emily was waiting for her. She stood by her front door, her crutches held close against her sides. It was a pose she'd always taken. It made the crutches invisible at first to the casual observer. Carole wasn't sure that Emily even knew she did it.

Carole stopped the car and reached across the front seat to open the door for Emily, who hurried over and climbed in, pulling her crutches in after her. Emily closed the door and waved a quick good-bye to her mother, and they were on their way to Pine Hollow. Stopping at Emily's house meant a slight detour for Carole, but she was only too happy to give her friend a lift.

"I saw Callie last night," Carole said as she turned onto the street.

"You went to her house?"

"Yeah. I wanted to let her know that Fez is

back, and I also wanted to see how she was doing."

"And?"

"She was tired. So is Fez."

"Well, both of them are going to need a lot of work before they're in form again." Emily tossed her backpack over the seat to make more room for herself. She fastened her seat belt.

"And you're going to see that she gets it?" Carole teased.

"Sure. I'm glad to do it, too. It's going to be a satisfying project. See, Callie is going to do all the work and she's going to get better, and that'll make me look brilliant."

"I hadn't thought of it that way," said Carole.

"You would have if you'd seen how she was sweating yesterday. She was working hard. I'm not surprised she was tired last night. I may be kidding about taking all the credit, but I'm not kidding about the fact that she'll get better. Maybe not a hundred percent. But better. I've spent a lot of time at handicapped riding centers. Everybody's there for a different reason, and everybody gets better in different ways. Callie will, too."

Carole kept her eyes on the road, driving calmly and confidently. "Does that bother you?" she asked.

"Does what bother me?" Emily asked.

Carole wondered if she should be asking this question, but she'd started and now she wasn't sure she could get out of it anyway. She proceeded.

"Does it bother you knowing that Callie will get better . . . and you won't?"

"You don't beat around the bush, do you?"

"You've always said you didn't want any special treatment or extra consideration," Carole reminded her. "I'm just asking a question."

"And an honest one," Emily said. "So I'll give you an honest answer. Of course it bothers me that I'll never get better. I wouldn't be normal if I didn't want to *be* normal. I'd love it if nobody ever stared at me or if nobody ever asked if they could help me just because they felt sorry for me. I wish I looked like everybody else. I wish I walked like everybody else. I wish I didn't have to see doctors all the time. I wish my parents didn't have to worry about me and that I didn't have to think about things like stairs, curbs, and sidewalks. I wish I could take gym just like my classmates—that nobody ever thought of me as different from anybody else."

"Oh, Emily, I'm sorry—I never thought—"

"I know you didn't, Carole, and that's one of

the things I like about you and our other friends. You *don't* think. I mean, you don't think about me as a handicapped friend. You think of me as a friend first and then as a rider, and then as maybe a classmate or a competitor. You think of me as someone who helps around the stable, someone you can laugh with or maybe rely on or borrow money from sometimes. And somewhere, way down the line, you think of me as being handicapped. That's a kind of thoughtlessness I can live with. Thank you for it."

"Do I say, 'You're welcome'?"

"If you want to." Emily laughed. "We've never really talked about this much and that's okay, but I don't mind talking about it. My handicap is part of me and I'm part of it. We are one, you see. Not everybody agrees with me, but the way I see it, I can do most of the things I want to do, and there are a lot of people without obvious handicaps who can't do some of the things I do—like, for instance, ride horses. In my case, it seems to me that the most disabling handicap I can have is in my head. I mean, at a certain point, handicaps are more in your head than they are in your muscles or your neurons or wherever they happen to be physically. It's important to know when to ask for help and when to take care of something yourself. When I can't tell the difference, that's when I'm really handicapped."

Carole didn't know what to say. She hadn't expected so much of an answer to her question.

"Glad you asked?" Emily teased.

"I guess so. I was just thinking about Callie . . ."

"I guess I didn't answer that part of the question. No, it doesn't bother me at all that Callie will get better. It makes me very happy to know that we'll be seeing progress there even if it takes a long time."

"All the more reason to work hard at helping her, I guess."

"I guess," Emily said.

Carole turned into the drive at Pine Hollow and parked her car. It was still early in the morning. A couple of the riders who liked to ride before work were out in the paddock. As the girls entered the stable, Carole saw that Ben and Red were working together to see that the horses were all fed and watered and the stalls given a quick morning cleanup.

"Let's go see our new patient," Carole said. They walked along the aisle, as Carole had the night before with Judy, greeting the horses on the way. Because of their conversation, Carole found herself more aware of the regular thumps of Emily's crutches than she remembered ever being before.

Fez was standing when they reached him. He'd made the effort to get up to be fed and watered. As soon as he'd eaten and drunk, he let himself back down and laid his head on the fresh hay, clearly relieved.

"There's a lot of work to be done here, isn't there?" Emily asked.

"A lot," Carole agreed. "Judy isn't sure he's going to make it. Ben seems convinced he can do it. I'm going to help all I can."

"We'll all pitch in," Emily said.

"Thanks," said Carole. "I've got to get to the office now. I'll see you later."

Carole stowed her lunch in the refrigerator and sat down at the desk, ready to start her day with the usual task of assigning horses and ponies. Something else had to be done first, though, because the light was blinking on the answering machine. She took up a pencil and a pad of paper and pressed Play.

"Max, it's Justin Waller over at the Horsemen's Association. We've received your reference letter, but we haven't heard from that young man yet. He's going to have to submit his application and project within the next two weeks. He knows about the deadline, doesn't he?"

Carole felt as though she'd heard something she wasn't supposed to. On the other hand, it was her job to listen to messages and relay them to Max. She made a note about the call and left it on Max's desk. But what was she going to do? What *could* she do?

Ben only had two weeks to complete his project. Two weeks to save Fez. What if it didn't work? It could mean the end of Ben's college career before it even started. That would be horrible. Carole wished she could talk with Ben about this, but since Ben generally seemed reluctant to discuss anything—from what kind of sandwich he'd brought for lunch to why she couldn't drive him home—it was going to be up to her to find out what she could on her own, in addition to helping him. For perhaps the hundredth time, she wished Ben were less secretive, more open, friendlier, easier to get along with— in sum, more like Scott. Or did she? That was something she'd take the time to consider at greater length when she didn't have a stack of mail to open and three lists of classes, all of which needed horse assignments.

She pulled the mail over first and picked up the sterling silver horse-head letter opener. Amused, she opened the first piece of mail.

"You May Already Be a Winner!" boldly proclaimed the envelope. Inside, the letter began, "Dear Mr. Hollow, If the number appearing . . ."

". . . in the garbage," Carole declared, and dropped it there.

Next came a bill from the feed supplier, copies of blood test results that needed to be filed, and then a postcard. Carole examined the photograph—stunningly stark hills silhouetted against a clear blue sky. It looked like California. Curious, she turned the card over. It *was* California. The card was from Lisa, addressed to "All my friends at Pine Hollow."

Now, this was much more interesting than the possibility of winning ten million dollars.

I'm having a great time out here in California and I wish you all could see what I'm up to. I've got a job—the best kind in the world, working with horses. My boss is much easier going than a lot of other stable owners (dig, dig!) . . . The horses are nice, too. It's all Western riding, which is quite a change, but change is good sometimes.

I think of you guys a lot and hope your summer is going well. For me, it's nothing but blue skies and horses. Give hugs to Prancer, Belle, Starlight, Barq, Penny,

Nickel, Comanche—oh, and some people,
too.

Love,
Lisa

Carole read the card three times and then dutifully got up and walked down the aisle of the stable, greeting all the horses Lisa had named and wondering how her summer was *really* going. Well, what could be wrong with being in California and being around horses and blue— Oh, of course, Lisa meant she was working with Skye!

Carole returned to her desk and set the postcard out prominently so that she wouldn't forget to show it to everyone who came in. Lisa knew everybody at the stable, and everybody would want to know how things were going— and if she wished they were there.

Lisa's parents had divorced several years before, and her father had moved to California and remarried. Most of the time since then, Lisa had lived with her mother, though she visited her father on school vacations. This year she was spending the entire summer out West. Carole and Stevie missed her terribly, and Stevie's twin brother missed her even more. Alex and Lisa had been going together for almost a year.

While Carole and Stevie were, at some level, convinced that Lisa was going to decide she liked it better in California and would never want to come back, Alex had added to that the notion that she was going to fall in love with someone else out there and would never want to see him again. Nothing Lisa had been able to say before she'd left had allayed his fears, and nothing in this postcard would help, either.

Carole guessed that the reference to blue skies in the postcard was a code of sorts. Years earlier the three girls had met and made friends with Skye Ransom. A lot of people were surprised that they claimed friendship with such a famous actor—heartthrob of American girls and of quite a few girls elsewhere throughout the world—but it was true. Over the years, the four of them had managed to get together occasionally and had maintained their friendship. Sometimes it was by phone, sometimes by e-mail or fax. More than a few times, the girls had gotten messages from Skye via production assistants. Skye did most of his work on the West Coast, but when his filming schedule brought him to the East, he always managed to meet up with The Saddle Club.

He was friends with all three of them, but there was a special bond between Skye and Lisa, and this was the basis for Alex's case of nerves about Lisa's summer away. His fears were heightened by the fact that Lisa had managed to get a job on the set of the television show Skye starred in. The show involved horses, and Lisa was an assistant stable hand.

"Hey, what's up?" asked a familiar voice from the office doorway.

Carole smiled and looked up from the card, which she was rereading. Stevie stood there, amused by Carole's total concentration.

"Lisa's up," Carole answered, waving the card. "She's written to all of us—well, everyone here at Pine Hollow. She's having fun."

Stevie stepped forward and took the proffered postcard. She read it quickly, shaking her head.

"Oh, no. She's never going to come back," she said.

Carole frowned. "Where'd you get that?"

"It's clear as can be. Look, she's having a wonderful time with the horses. You know what the blue skies are, right?"

"I got that," Carole said.

"And she likes her boss better than she likes Max."

"I don't think she really meant that," said Carole.

"Sure, she's being funny about it now, but we won't be laughing when the end of August comes and there's no sign of her. She'll be in

Hollywood High School before you can say boo."

"I don't think so. Her father's house is fifty miles from Hollywood!" Carole said.

"Well, whatever. You know what I mean."

"Look, Lisa left here without any intention of staying there. She'll be back." Carole said that very definitely, but she didn't really feel definite. Lisa was having a good time. She was probably having a better time than Carole was, and she was definitely having a better time than Stevie was. Why would she want to come home?

"Good morning!" Callie greeted the girls cheerfully. They had been so deep in thought that they hadn't heard her at all. "What's that?" she asked.

"A postcard from Lisa," Stevie said, passing it to her.

Callie glanced at the message and then turned the card over. She sighed.

"Sounds like she's having fun, doesn't it?" Carole asked.

"I guess so. I was looking at the picture, though. It reminds me of home. It's so beautiful there."

"It's beautiful here, too," Stevie said defensively.

"Yes, but it's a different beautiful there, and I miss it."

"Lisa's really something," said Stevie. "With one cheery postcard, she's managed to upset almost everybody at Pine Hollow."

"Absence can be powerful," Callie observed. There was a moment of silence while Stevie and Carole absorbed that thought. "And speaking of absence, I'm going to go say hello to Fez before my session. How's he doing this morning?"

"He seemed about the same when I looked in on him earlier. Oh, Emily is here. She's all set to work with you whenever you're ready."

"Thanks," said Callie. She made her way out of the office and down the aisle toward Fez's stall. The uneven thump of her crutches seemed to echo off the high ceilings.

Carole opened her desk drawer, found a pushpin, and handed it to Stevie to post Lisa's card on the bulletin board in the locker area.

Stevie worked her way through the milling crowd of eight-year-olds who were waiting for their pony assignments. She welcomed the noise, even the whining. Absence was powerful, and distraction was good.

SIX

Stevie looked around her at the melee in the locker area. Eager young riders were trying to sort out socks, jackets, hats, riding crops, and boot hooks. It didn't seem so long ago that she'd been one of them. She shook her head. At seventeen, she was much too young to be sentimental, no matter how tempting it was. She also couldn't avoid seeing Fez forever. It was time.

She left the locker area and walked down the aisle to Fez's stall. Callie was there, peering over the doorway, and Emily stood next to her. Stevie joined them.

"Wow! Look at that!" she said when she peeked over the door.

Ben was in the stall with Fez. The horse was standing up, and Ben was grooming him. Fez was cross-tied, but he was also tied up in a lot of other ways.

"It's a sling," Callie explained. "Well, sort of."

59

And it was: a body sling. The horse was supported by a web of leather and nets that was suspended from the roof beams and slung under his belly. The sling wasn't holding his full weight, but it was taking enough of the weight off the damaged leg—as well as off the others— to allow Fez to remain upright.

"The idea here is to make him use his leg a little, but not a lot," said Emily.

"I couldn't teach him to hold crutches properly," said Ben, regarding his audience wryly.

"You were waiting for Emily and me to be here to try that line, weren't you?" Callie asked.

"A-yep," Ben admitted. He continued grooming the horse. It wasn't easy to do because the leather and the nylon netting interfered with a normal grooming, but he was doing the best he could, and Fez seemed to be benefitting both from the extra attention and from standing up.

"How long is he going to stay in that thing?" Stevie asked.

"Not long," said Ben. "Just another few minutes. Then some more later on today and some tomorrow, too. A little more each day until he builds up strength, and then less each day after that because he won't need it anymore."

"Is that all he's going to need to get better?" Stevie asked.

"Nope."

It was a dumb question and got the dumb answer it deserved. Stevie shook her head. Of course the horse would need a lot more than that. As soon as he could walk securely, there would be some sort of exercise regimen to build his muscles. And if Ben had put half as much thought into the exercise scheme as he had the sling, it was going to be great.

Fez was standing still for his grooming, but it wasn't as if he had much choice. He was immobilized by both the sling and his injuries. When Stevie focused her attention on him, she realized that he was a good deal sicker than he appeared, standing so politely—and necessarily—still. While Ben groomed him, his head hung low, his ears flopped disinterestedly, and his eyes seemed dull. His tail hung listlessly. Most of his feed from the morning remained in his pail. This was a sick horse.

Stevie tried to suppress the memory of Fez before the accident. She'd looked after him a bit. She'd even ridden him. He had been spirited to the point of sassiness; he had been stubborn, proud, and full of heart. He hadn't made it easy for whoever was in his saddle, but the rewards of riding him well had been great. Stevie knew he'd earned a cabinetful of ribbons on countless endurance courses. An endurance specialist was a special horse indeed. Now the light seemed to be gone from his eyes, the spirit from his heart.

"Okay, that's enough for now," said Ben. Methodically he removed all the leather straps and the netting, allowing Fez to ease down into the straw.

"Looks like he's ready for his morning nap," said Emily. "So I guess we have to get to work."

She stood back from the stall door, letting Ben out. Callie followed her across the hall to where PC was waiting patiently, tacked up and ready for his lesson.

Ben helped Callie into the saddle and opened the gate for her, PC, and Emily to go into the small schooling ring where they'd worked the day before. He then returned to Fez's stall and began folding up the sling. Stevie held the straps while he arranged the netting and untangled some of the hooks. They stepped back outside the stall.

"He's still a fine horse," Ben said, as if reading Stevie's mind.

She didn't answer. There really wasn't any need to.

"He's got heart. Always has," Ben added. "That's the most important thing."

"It may not be enough," said Stevie.

"No, it may not be," said Ben.

"And it's my fault," said Stevie.

"Maybe," said Ben. "Maybe not. Maybe you couldn't help it. One thing, though . . ."

"What?"

"He is—or was—a great horse by any measure, but the finest horse in the world isn't worth the lives of three people."

"I—Uh—" Stevie began to speak, to try to respond, but Ben didn't expect a response. Without another word, he swung the stall door closed, latched it, picked up the empty water bucket, and walked away, leaving Stevie alone with her thoughts, not necessarily more comforting for his words to her.

She walked down the aisle in the opposite direction, toward Belle's stall. As usual, Belle recognized her footsteps long before she could possibly have seen Stevie, and stuck her head up over her stall door. Her ears flicked alertly. She tossed her head eagerly. Stevie could hardly help smiling.

"I suppose you think there's some sort of treat for you in my pocket," she said, approaching the horse.

Belle's answer was to nuzzle Stevie's neck and nip at her hair.

"I know, I know. I didn't brush it well enough this morning and it looks like hay, but it's not," Stevie said, standing back. Belle continued to tug playfully at it. "Talk about a cure for split ends," Stevie said, tugging back and, finally, wresting a lock of hair from the horse's teeth. She dug in her pocket and found some carrot chunks, which Belle seemed to like even more than hair. While the mare chewed, Stevie hugged her. Really, the only time she could hug Belle safely was when the mare's teeth were occupied with something other than her hair. And Stevie had to hug Belle now. It was the only way she could be sure she was hiding her tears if somebody came down the aisle. It was both odd and wonderful that the horse could be so oblivious to Stevie's unhappiness. That alone was comforting.

Stevie slipped into the stall, seeking more comfort and some privacy. Somehow, when things didn't make sense, she'd found the simple pleasure of being with a horse clarifying. She breathed deeply, loving the familiar scents of horse and hay blended with leather and grain. And she cried, uncontrollably.

"And you get Patch today," Carole told the little girl on the other side of the desk.

"Pa-atch!" the little girl whined.

"Or you can sit on the side and watch the other riders," Carole said threateningly.

"Okay, Patch," the girl agreed, walking out of the office glumly.

"What was that all about?" Max asked Carole as he walked in.

"This is the class where everybody wants to ride Nickel and nobody wants to ride Patch," Carole said. "It has something to do with one of the girls getting her finger nipped when she gave Patch a piece of apple at the beginning of the spring term. Ever since then, there is nothing Patch can do to redeem his reputation with this group."

Max laughed. Young riders were often silly in how they chose their horses.

"We were never that bad, were we?" she asked.

"I plead the Fifth," Max said.

"Oh, dear."

"But the good news is that I'm not teaching that class today. Red is taking it for me. I've got a humongous stack of paperwork, as you can see because it's mostly sitting on that desk, and I've got to get to it. I'll make you a deal, Carole. I'll cover the desk while I attack all this paperwork if you'll come back this afternoon and enter all the data in the computer. Denise will be busy with afternoon classes, and I always feel like a ham-handed idiot with that damn thing. Besides, you're so good with it."

"Flattery, Max? *You're* reduced to flattery?"

"That's one way of looking at it," he conceded. "But isn't there something else you'd rather be doing right now?"

"You mean like going for a trail ride?" Carole asked.

"Perhaps. Speaking of which, I saw Stevie lurking around Belle's stall. Think that might do her some good, too?" he asked.

"I suspect it might do her a world of good," Carole said. "Thanks, Max. I'll make it up to you."

"You bet," he said. "On the computer later today. I'm going to need my glasses, and I left them in the house. I'll be right back."

Carole tidied up the horse-and-rider charts and set them aside. She'd finished that task for the morning classes, and there was no need to clutter the desk with them. She put away her pencils, pads, and erasers and dumped six paper clips into the cup on the desk.

Carole was at the stable manager's desk in the mornings. In the afternoon the job was done by Denise McCaskill, a graduate student in equine studies who was also Red O'Malley's girlfriend. Carole and Denise had made a deal that no matter how messy the desk got during a shift, it would always be neat at the end. Carole was doing her part.

She was almost done with her tidying when Scott Forester stepped into the office.

"Is Callie here?" he asked.

"Sure," Carole said. "She should be in the small schooling ring with Emily." Then, realizing that Scott wouldn't know a schooling ring from a paddock, she explained, "The place where they were riding yesterday."

"Right," he said. "I just wanted to make sure she's okay."

"She's okay," Carole promised. "Nobody here will let anything bad happen to her."

"Thanks. And, um, I wanted to remind folks about the barbecue. My mom and dad want to be sure everybody knows they're welcome . . ."

"I think they made that clear yesterday," Carole said. "But if you want, we could put a notice on the board."

"Okay," he said. "Good idea." Carole handed him some paper and a box of colored pens so that he could make up the invitation. He sat in the visitor's chair, facing Carole, and began making a colorful poster.

Carole expected Max to reappear, so she wasn't surprised when she heard heavy male footsteps at the door. It wasn't Max, though. It was Ben. He stepped into the office, opened his mouth as if to say something to Carole, and then, spotting Scott, withdrew.

Carole turned her eyes to Scott, who was working earnestly to devise a clever, welcoming invitation. Even with just a set of colored markers, Scott could manage to be warm, funny, and inviting. What a contrast that was to Ben Marlow!

In a few minutes the task was done. Carole handed Scott a pushpin and pointed to the locker area, assuring him that she'd be at the barbecue on Saturday. Max reappeared then, glasses in hand, with a stony look that told her exactly how much he was looking forward to a couple of hours' worth of paperwork. She was convinced that the smartest place to be while he was grumbling at papers was very far away indeed.

She took a detour past the tack room, picked up Starlight's tack, and went in search of Stevie. Not surprisingly, she found her friend in Belle's stall.

"I've been given a Get Out of Jail Free card. Want to go on a trail ride?"

Stevie squeezed her eyes shut, trying both to

clear them of the tears that had so lately filled them and to clear her mind. Carole had startled her, and she'd been so deep in thought that she wasn't sure she'd heard right.

"Trail ride?" she echoed. *Right.* She knew what that was. Did she want to go on a trail ride? No, she wanted to remain lost in Belle's stall for a long time, undiscovered, invisible, and alone.

"I figured it was time we checked out the creek. On a hot day like this, our feet could use some cool water."

Willow Creek ran through the woods behind Pine Hollow. As long as the girls had been riding at the stable, they'd had a favorite place by the creek. The horses could have a drink there, and the girls could dangle their feet in the water, which seemed icy even on the hottest day of the summer.

"Trail ride?" Stevie said again.

"Right, like with horses," Carole teased.

Carole needs to talk, Stevie thought. And besides, she couldn't hide behind Belle forever. She'd have to come out sometime. Now was as good a time as any.

"Great," Stevie said. "I'll just finish grooming Belle and then I can tack her up. I'll meet you at the good-luck horseshoe in fifteen minutes."

"Deal," said Carole, stepping back from the

stall door. She proceeded down the aisle to Starlight's stall, too polite to mention to her best friend that if she was having any trouble grooming Belle, it might be because her grooming bucket was still in the aisle.

SEVEN

Carole breathed deeply. The warm air was pleasantly tinged with the scent of horses and the inviting smell of the piney woods that lay beyond the field. It was summer and she was riding her horse, so what could be wrong with the world? All her life, she'd found an almost unbearable joy in the simple fact of horses. As a little girl, people had sometimes teased her that she'd outgrow horses as soon as she discovered boys. She'd smiled at the teasing, knowing that horses were different for her than they were for the *temporarily* horse-crazy girls. Her insanity was permanent. In time she had discovered boys, too, and she liked them just fine—not better than horses, but differently. She leaned forward in the saddle and patted Starlight. He flicked his ears in appreciation and then, when she nudged his belly, broke into a trot.

Behind her, Stevie followed suit. It was an easy and natural change. The fresh air was invigorating, and a walk wouldn't do in the charged atmosphere.

Soon they left the open fields that surrounded Pine Hollow and entered the woods on a well-traveled trail. The woods behind the stable were crisscrossed with trails, well known to all the riders, and each one had a favorite. One trail passed an old abandoned farmhouse; one went near the quarry. One went straight through, coming out near the center of the little town of Willow Creek. Another led to a maze of trails, all of which ascended to the top of the wooded hill. Best of all, however, was the one that circled the hill and led to the creek.

The horses slowed to a walk as they approached the creek. The burbling of the water invited them forward, and without any signal from their riders, they halted. Starlight and Belle knew what was up even if Carole and Stevie weren't telling them. The girls dismounted and tied their horses where they could reach the cool water.

Carole and Stevie shed their boots and socks and scootched across the wide rock that bordered the creek, taking up their traditional foot-dunking positions. Carole hiked her breeches up her legs, and Stevie did the same with her jeans. Carole reached forward and tested the rushing water with her fingers. Stevie wasn't so tentative.

She just plunged her feet into the water. The cool rush surprised her, as it always did, and then comforted her, as it always did. Carole pulled her fingers out and put her feet in.

"Aaaaahhh," she sighed.

"Me too," said Stevie.

"I know you're having a hard time," Carole began.

"I wasn't crying," said Stevie.

"I know," Carole lied.

"I was just grooming Belle."

"She looks great," Carole said. She leaned forward and looked into the clear water of the creek. She pointed to a small school of minnows facing into the gentle current. Stevie sat up and watched them.

"They're so tiny," she said.

"Their world is pretty tiny, too," said Carole.

"I guess," Stevie said, leaning back on the flat rock. "I got another job, you know."

"You're not going back to Pizza Manor?" Stevie had loved her pizza delivery job. "Didn't your parents get you and Alex a new car with the insurance money?"

"Yes, but I think Pizza Manor replaced me already. Besides, now I'm working at the laundry."

"The one at the shopping center?"

Stevie nodded. "I can walk to it, so Alex can

use the car all the time. And the good news is that it's really boring. The manager said I was good at measuring detergent. Now she lets me sell fabric softener, too. Next week—who knows?—maybe bleach."

"Well, there's a career move for you," Carole teased.

Stevie winced. Carole realized that her friend wasn't in the mood to be teased and wished she could take back the words.

"There must be something more interesting you could do. Maybe even at Pine Hollow?"

"I asked Max," Stevie said. "He was really nice about it, and he'll let me fill in sometimes, but he doesn't need another person working there. Everything else that was available required a car or a ride—you know, like something at the mall."

"But you could use the car," Carole said.

"I haven't, you know."

"You haven't . . . ?"

"I haven't driven since the accident," Stevie said.

"Oh," said Carole. She hadn't realized; she hadn't even thought about it. Stevie had loved driving. She'd gotten a job that required driving on the first day she had her license. How could she have stopped driving?

74

"I hurt two people I care about and a valuable horse," Stevie went on.

"It wasn't your fault," Carole countered.

"That's what everyone says, but they weren't there."

"I was."

"Not driving."

"No, but I was in the car, and you saved my life."

"I should have pulled over when it started to rain like that. I couldn't see."

"You didn't have time to pull over. One second it wasn't raining, the next second it was a deluge. We're all lucky you handled it as well as you did. We could all be dead—including Fez. That's good news, Stevie, nothing to mope about."

"The only good news about the whole situation was that the car was so bashed in that I never had to confess to Alex or my parents that I'd dented it the week before."

"You'd dented it?" Carole sat up and looked at Stevie. "Badly?"

"Pretty much," said Stevie. "I broke a taillight and smashed the rear bumper."

"What a cover-up!" Carole said, beginning to giggle.

Stevie sat up, too. "Maybe a little extreme?"

"Not a bit," Carole said.

Stevie began giggling, too. "I was really worried about that dent."

"And now nobody will ever know," Carole said.

"Alex would have been furious."

"He's none the wiser."

"My father would have made me pay the deductible."

"Think how much money you saved."

"My mother would have grounded me."

"And you're free as a bird," said Carole. "See? We found the silver lining."

"There had to be one somewhere," said Stevie. "But it gives all that darkness a tiny bright side."

"Just between us," said Carole.

"Definitely," said Stevie.

They shook hands.

"Am I supposed to give you a lecture now about getting back on the horse when you fall off?"

"No," said Stevie. "We both know that only means when you're not too badly hurt to ride. I'm still too badly hurt. I'm not ready to drive yet."

"If you want, I'll let you drive my car," Carole offered.

"With you in it?"

"Of course," said Carole.

"Maybe," said Stevie. It wasn't the answer Carole had hoped for, but it was the best answer Stevie was ready to make. As long as Carole had known her, Stevie had always been a girl who knew her own mind. When she was ready, she'd be ready—not before.

"So now that we've covered what's on my mind, what's up with you?" Stevie asked. "You seem concerned about something more than me and Callie and Fez. Not that we aren't all enough to make you pull your hair out."

"I didn't think anyone had noticed," said Carole.

"So?"

"Working at Pine Hollow is great," Carole began. "I feel so lucky to be around all the wonderful horses and the people, doing exactly what I've always wanted to do."

Stevie waited. Carole didn't offer any more. This was going to take some prompting. "So?" Stevie repeated.

Carole swallowed and then spoke. "It's Ben. He's so difficult to get along with."

"You mean he makes things hard around the stable?"

"No, no. Not that at all. He's a wonderful worker, and he's almost magical with the horses. They all love him. It's just that he's so—oh, I don't know—annoying? He does more grunting than talking. One minute we'll be having what passes for a conversation, like when we were working together in Fez's stall the other day, and then the next, it's as if we've never met. He gets all sullen and slinks around. Like, before you came this morning, Scott showed up. He was in my office, asking about Callie and Fez. Ben walks in, sees Scott, and turns around and walks out without saying anything. Now you and I both know that Ben doesn't come into the office for exercise. He had something to say, but is he too shy to talk in front of two people at once? Am I expected to run after him to beg him to tell me what's on his mind? Am I supposed to be at his beck and call all the time?"

"Carole!" Stevie exclaimed.

"Well, maybe it's not that bad. But he's so glum!"

"You think he's being glum?"

"What would you call it?"

"You don't know?"

"Know what?"

"He's interested in you, Carole. At least, that's what I think."

"He's only interested in horses."

"He's a guy. Guys tend to be interested in girls no matter what else they're interested in," said Stevie.

"Ben? Are you kidding?"

"No, I'm not kidding. Don't you see that he's jealous of Scott? I mean, well, who wouldn't be? Scott's terrifically good looking, he talks easily with everyone and anyone—except me—and Ben feels like a klutz around him. Scott flirts the way some people breathe."

"Not with me," Carole protested.

"With everyone, including you. He oozes charm and charisma. It's only natural for people to treat him the same way in return. Oh, yes, he flirts with you, and it doesn't mean any more to him than it does when he flirts with me or even his sister. He's simply a nice, easygoing guy. This upsets Ben, who is just one of those two things. Nice, I mean. Not easygoing."

"That doesn't make any sense, Stevie."

"Who said it had to? I could be wrong about Ben being interested in you, but I'm not wrong about him envying Scott's approach to life."

"Maybe he's irritated by it."

"No difference there," said Stevie.

"Well, it seems to me that Ben Marlow is irritated by far too many things."

"Some people have good reasons for being upset about things," said Stevie.

"Like what?" Carole challenged her.

"Oh, I don't know. We don't really know anything at all about Ben, do we?"

"We know he's good with horses."

Stevie laughed in spite of herself. It was like Carole to value that trait so highly that it would be enough for her to judge a whole person. "Sure, there's that," she said. "But he never lets anybody know anything else about him. Like the other day, Ben and I were mucking out a stall together and I got to talking about school and I asked him where he'd gone to high school. He actually changed the subject to grain mixtures, and although I didn't think much about it at the time, I realized later he'd been evading the question. What's the big deal about where he went to school?"

"Hmmm," said Carole. "Hey, maybe it's time to get back to the stable."

"Are you changing the subject on me?" Stevie teased.

"About as effectively as you did on me," Carole countered.

"Touché." Stevie withdrew her feet from the cool creek and shook them dry before pulling on her socks and boots. Carole did the same. A few minutes later, both girls were ready to ride. They mounted up and began the return journey to Pine Hollow.

The trail ride and the pause by the creek had been just what each of them had needed. They'd needed to talk, though not to resolve anything. Now their visit was finished and once again they rode quietly, exchanging few words.

Carole thought over what Stevie had said. She dismissed the idea that Ben was interested in her as being a fabrication of Stevie's hyperactive imagination, but she knew Stevie was right that at some level Ben envied Scott. Who wouldn't? And what else was there to know about Ben?

Her mind was working on these thoughts as they emerged from the woods and entered the fields that surrounded Pine Hollow. There was often a magical quality about being in the woods, as if they defined another world where everything was protected, safe, different. The glaring sun that greeted them when they came out of the trees made it hard to see. Carole, in the lead, drew Starlight to a halt and waited for her eyes to adjust. Stevie came up next to her, blinking.

"What's up?" Stevie asked.

"It's always like returning to reality," Carole said, sharing her feelings about the woods and the field.

"No, I mean over there," said Stevie, pointing to Pine Hollow.

Something was up. There was a knot of people at one end of the schooling ring. That wasn't normal. Usually there were hardly any people who weren't on horses.

"Something's wrong," Carole said. Simultaneously they brought their horses to a canter and sped across the fields, constantly watching the crowd in the distance, trying to see what was happening.

It was an accident, that was for sure. Somebody had been hurt—otherwise there was no way that clump of people would remain. Then the riders saw the blinking of an emergency light. An ambulance?

It was, and it had been there for a while; it was leaving now, speeding along the driveway and then disappearing along the road that ran next to the stable. The knot of people had almost completely dispersed by the time Carole and Stevie reached the paddock.

Max was there, along with Emily. They stood talking. PC waited patiently beside them. They looked up when Carole and Stevie reached them.

"What happened?" Stevie asked.

"It's Callie," Emily said. "She fell off PC. She hurt her other leg and they've taken her to the hospital again. I didn't mean to let it happen."

"You didn't let it happen," said Max. "She fell. People fall off horses all the time. It's just that Callie's balance was more affected than any of us, including Callie, realized. She'll be okay."

"I hope so," said Emily.

The sharpness in her tone reminded Carole of the conversation they'd had earlier that day. This day was too full of serious conversations for her taste.

Ben appeared out of the shadows of the stable. "I'll walk 'em for you," he said, reaching for Starlight's and Belle's reins. Carole and Stevie readily relinquished their horses to his care.

"Come on. I'll drive you guys home," Carole said to Stevie and Emily. For once they were both ready to leave Pine Hollow for the day. Even Carole, who had to come back later to keep her promise to Max, suddenly needed some time away.

EIGHT

"I have to go see her."

"Stevie, are you sure that's such a great idea?" Phil asked. The two of them were sitting in Phil's car, parked in Stevie's driveway. Phil had come over to see Stevie, but before he could get out of his car, she'd gotten in and asked him to take her to Callie's house.

"Well, you don't have to drive me or anything. It's just a couple of blocks away and I can walk."

"It's not that and you know it," Phil said, taking her hand. "You've been torturing yourself over what happened—not that that isn't a pretty natural thing to do. But you don't have to rub salt in your own wounds, do you?"

"I have to go see her," Stevie repeated. "She's home from the emergency room. Her mother said so. I just want to check in. I feel like . . ."

"Like you have to?"

"Yeah, like I have to," Stevie agreed. "So it'll be better if you're there with me, okay?"

"Okay," Phil said, relenting. He shifted his car into gear and backed out of the driveway. As long as he'd known Stevie—and he'd known her a long time—she'd always been the most stubborn person he'd ever met. When she got an idea into her head, no matter how wrong it was, it was almost impossible to get her to change her mind. It wasn't that she never changed her mind; she did that all the time. She just never let anyone else change it for her. Or if they did, she wouldn't let them know they'd done it. It wasn't Phil's favorite aspect of Stevie's personality.

In this case, though, he thought he understood it. Because Stevie had been behind the wheel when Callie had gotten hurt, he knew she felt responsible at some level for the accident. But now, even more simply, she felt responsible for seeing that everything possible was done for Callie.

This wasn't easy. She had no problem with the idea of Emily's and PC's working with the girl; it was such a good idea that she might even have convinced herself it was her own. The hard part was interacting with Callie and with her family. Every legal document in the world exonerated her. Every logical argument pointed to the obvious conclusion that she had taken all the appropriate steps to minimize the damage in the crash. Yet every beat of her heart told her there must have been something more she could have done, and she was convinced that everybody else felt the same way—most especially Callie's family. Phil thought that, in the case of Callie's brother, Stevie was right.

"Okay, here we are," Phil said, pulling up in front of the Foresters'. Stevie reached for the car door handle, but Phil caught hold of her hand. He looked right into her eyes. "I'm with you now, and I'll be with you when we leave," he said. He leaned forward and kissed her softly on the lips.

She kissed him back and thanked him. Then she opened the car door. She had her courage.

When Mrs. Forester came to the door, Stevie explained that she'd just wanted to stop by to see how Callie was doing.

"Well, come see for yourself," said Mrs. Forester, inviting them in.

Callie was ensconced in what was obviously her father's recliner. Her crutches were propped on the armrest, and her left leg was swathed in bandages.

"Oh, Callie!" said Stevie, distressed at the sight.

Callie immediately sat up in the chair and used the bandaged leg to lower the footrest.

"Don't take this too seriously," she said. "It's just a bruise, really. The doctor said something about how the hospital was having a special on elastic bandages, so he gave me two. Believe me, it looks a lot worse than it feels."

"You're kidding, right?" Stevie asked, settling onto a nearby chair.

"I'm kidding about the special on elastic bandages," Callie said. "But I'm not kidding that it looks worse than it feels. It's really not a big deal. No brain damage. In fact, the only thing that really got damaged was my dignity. Like, I wanted to be carted out of Pine Hollow in an ambulance? Trust me, though, the good-luck horseshoe was true to itself. This is not a serious matter."

"Promise?"

"Scout's honor," Callie said. Stevie suspected that at some level Callie was just trying to make her feel better, but she was also pleased to note that it was working.

Mrs. Forester appeared then with a tray of homemade cookies and a bottle of soda. Callie's father and Scott walked in, following the scented trail of cookies. Congressman Forester greeted Stevie and Phil warmly. Scott shook Phil's hand and nodded a cool greeting to

Stevie. They weren't fooling one another. The charming and charismatic Scott Forester was unable to display his usual warmth and openness to the girl who had been driving when his sister got hurt.

"So, the way I see it, this is kind of a good news/bad news situation," Callie said.

"How's that?" asked Phil.

"Well, for a couple of weeks, I've been complaining about how difficult it is to manage when one side of me works and the other doesn't. Those days are over. Now neither side of me works. I know I'm joking about it, but it might actually make it a little easier to ride—when I can ride again, which I think will be tomorrow—to get back up on the horse and all that. PC is so willing and so easy to manage that I could probably ride him if I were completely paralyzed. Which I'm not. And, anyway, the important thing is that the doctor said I'd be able to swim, and we're going to need to do that at the party." She turned to Phil. "Stevie told you about it, right? And you're coming, right?"

"Right on both counts," he said. "I'll be here. Thanks for including me."

Phil stood up, and so did Stevie. They'd done what they'd come for—made sure Callie was okay. Now it was time to go.

"See you on Saturday—if not before," said

Stevie. She and Phil thanked Callie's parents, thanking Mrs. Forester specially for the cookies, said good-bye to Scott, and left. When they got back into Phil's car, he squeezed Stevie's hand.

"You were right," he said. "It was the right thing to do."

"I know," said Stevie. "She has a way of making me feel better no matter how bad I know she feels. If only her brother . . ."

"He'll get over it eventually."

"I hope eventually is soon."

Carole shook her head in annoyance and glared at the computer screen. Bright colors and cheerful-looking prompts weren't going to make this onerous task any easier. The file had to be set up just right before information went in or the data would be useless.

She was no genius when it came to the computer. She was merely better at using it than Max was, and that had been enough to earn her the right to tackle the task that now faced her. She'd been using computers at school and at home since she was a little girl. The machine sitting on her desk was the first one Max had ever used.

"Okay, look," she had said to Max. "We'll need to have data files . . ."

"As opposed to what other kind of files?" he had asked.

Not only did she have to figure out how to do it, but she'd had to figure out how to explain it. "Let me start again," she'd said.

It had taken her an hour to explain to Max what it was they needed to do, and then it had taken her another hour to do it—or at least to set it up. She was beginning to think she'd made a bad deal when she'd let Max do paperwork while she and Stevie went for their trail ride.

Finally, when the files were set up the way she and Max wanted them, she began entering information. That was the easy part. Max sat across from her at the desk, shuffling papers and paying bills.

On the other side of the door, the stable was settling down for the night. Red and Denise were long gone. Ben was bedding down the horses, checking their water and seeing to it that they had hay and that their stalls were clean for the night. When he was finished, he came into the office to check out.

"See you," he said, chatty as ever. Then he was gone.

Carole worked for another hour. The first file they were creating was a simple address file, including all the riders, owners, suppliers, and employees. The bigger task would come when they started creating files for each horse, replacing the notebooks that now filled the office shelves. It was a lot of data. Tonight's address list was a modest beginning, and once Carole was simply entering data, it wasn't very challenging. She and Max could chat while she worked.

"I stopped by Fez's stall earlier today," said Max.

"What do you think?" Carole asked.

"I think it's a miracle he's made it this far," he said. "I've talked to Judy about it. We both agree that we have to prepare for any eventuality here."

"But Ben's done so much!" Carole said.

"Ben's been doing good work with the horse," Max said. "No question about it. And Fez has benefitted from it, I'm sure. I don't like to think what would be happening with him if Ben weren't putting in so much effort. I just hope his good work comes to a good end."

"Well, Ben's made it a real project," said Carole. It occurred to her that this could be a good opportunity to ferret out more information about Ben and his plans for the future.

"Hmmm," Max said noncommittally while he licked an envelope.

Carole decided to try another tack. "Oh, did

you get that message from that man—Mr. Waller?—something about a reference?" she asked.

"Yes," said Max. He picked up another bill and checked the calculations on it.

"Was that about a scholarship or something?" she asked.

"Something," he answered.

Carole could tell she was being shut out. She knew when to stop asking questions, but the very existence of the unanswered questions made her all the more curious. What was it about Ben Marlow that was so mysterious? Why was he so secretive? Why wouldn't he ever talk about himself? Why wouldn't Max ever talk about him? This made her recall Stevie's absurd assertion that Ben was interested in her. Ben, sullen, quiet, withdrawn—the guy who could talk to horses but not to people. Carole smiled, thinking about that. Maybe she could understand it. In her life, no horse had ever disappointed her, let her down, or lied to her. When times were bleak, whether it had been during her mother's illness, tough periods in school, or any other hardship, she'd always found comfort in being with horses. Maybe she and Ben weren't so different after all.

"That's it for me for tonight," said Max. "I've pretty much emptied out the bank account, so I have to stop paying bills, and I'd better let you get home or your father's going to be after my hide for working you too hard!"

Carole laughed, then stretched. She got achy when she sat at a computer for long periods, and she was definitely feeling achy now. Max was right. It was time to stop for the night. Tomorrow would come soon enough.

"I'm just going to check on Fez before I turn out the lights," he said. "Care to go with me?"

"Sure," said Carole. She saved her work and printed a single record for herself, then closed the files and turned off the computer. She followed Max down the aisle to Fez's stall.

The horse was little changed. He was lying on the straw, his head resting and his ears limp. He opened his eyes when Carole and Max stood at his door, but he didn't lift his head or show any particular interest in them.

"I know Ben was working with him today," Carole said. She was trying to sound encouraging, though it wasn't clear whether it was for Ben's or Fez's benefit—or for that of both of them. "He's been working very hard with him."

Max shook his head, looking at the ailing horse. "I hope it's worth it," he said.

"Me too," said Carole.

She and Max finished turning out the lights,

and he saw her to her car, closing the door securely.

"Thanks for all your work, Carole. I'll see you in the morning."

"Bye," she said.

She watched Max amble to his house, then started her engine as he went inside. Before shifting the car into gear, she turned on the interior light and reached into her pocket for the record she'd printed.

> *Marlow, Benjamin, 273 Winn Road, Willow Creek, VA*

Winn Road. Carole was trying to remember where that was. It definitely wasn't in the neighborhood of Pine Hollow, nor was it anywhere near her own house. Carole and her father lived on the edge of town, several miles from Pine Hollow, far enough that she'd taken the bus or been taxied by her father in the days before she could drive.

Winn Road. Carole thought she recalled seeing something like that over by the old elementary school. She was curious and almost convinced herself that she was more curious to test her memory about where Winn Road was than to see where Ben lived. *You can learn a lot about a person from their house,* she reminded herself. She remembered how it felt to be in the Foresters' comfortable, welcoming house. Even from the outside, she'd liked it. How would she feel about Ben's?

She shifted the car into gear and pulled out onto the dark, quiet street that bordered Pine Hollow. This was the street where she and Callie and Stevie had had the accident. It was so different now. The summer sky was bright with stars. A fingernail moon shined softly. There was no threat anywhere.

Carole was right about Winn Road. It was a long way from Pine Hollow, perhaps two or three miles, and she knew enough about the local buses to know that none went near there. It probably took Ben more than half an hour to get to and from work each day, yet he'd refused a ride. What a curious person he was.

When Carole drove toward Winn Road, she had to relinquish any notion she'd been harboring of simply testing her knowledge of the local geography. She knew that she wanted to see where Ben lived. Winn Road was off Barlow Street. On Barlow, the houses were modest tract homes, close to one another. Each seemed to be very much like the one next to it, some with the front door to the right of the picture window, some to the left. Kids from the neighborhood were playing a game of basketball around a hoop on one of the small garages. Families sat on folding chairs in their front yards, enjoying the pleasant summer evening.

Carole turned onto Winn. This was an older street. The houses were small, filling cramped lots. One house had car parts scattered in the dirt that passed for a driveway. Another had a rusted jungle gym in the small front yard. A nondescript mutt barked loudly in his yard, where he was tied to a tree with a frayed rope. It was hard to see the numbers on the houses. A tilted mailbox in front of one home read 251. A little farther down, she found the number 263. She slowed down. Ben's house was near. This was Ben's street, with broken cars, rusted toys, untended dogs, and tilted mailboxes. Did she really want to know this?

Carole pulled to the curb across the street from the unnumbered house that had to be Ben Marlow's home. No one saw her stop. No one saw her turn off her engine and douse her lights. But she noticed a lot. She saw a house that was no better than its neighbors. It needed a coat of paint, and the front yard had long since relinquished its claim to grass. It was nearly bald dirt. There was no garage, but there was a rocky driveway. In it was a ten-year-old car with a broken taillight patched with red tape. To the side of the house was a laundry line, filled with clothes that must have been out there all day and were now getting wet all over again from the humid night air.

The windows of the house were covered by shades, but Carole could see there were lamps on downstairs and there was a dim welcome light on the porch, surrounded by curious insects. Somebody was home. Somebody was expected.

The front door opened, casting a beam of light across the empty front yard. Carole sat up, suddenly alert and wondering if Ben would be there.

It wasn't Ben, though. An old man walked out, thin and frail, struggling with a big plastic laundry basket. Father? *No, too old,* Carole thought. More likely a grandfather, but why would he be retrieving the laundry if Ben could do it?

She sat still in the car, guiltily watching the man tug at the underwear, shirts, and towels on the line. She could hardly offer to help him, but she could barely stand to watch. Where was Ben?

That question was answered when Ben came down the street from the opposite end, carrying two large brown bags. Carole recalled a small shopping area near the school. He must have gone for groceries—or picked them up on his way home from Pine Hollow.

Ben spotted the old man working on the laundry and hurriedly put the bags on the front step so that he could help with the laundry. While the man stood back and rested, Ben took all the clothes off the line and folded them with the same cool efficiency Carole knew so well from watching him work at Pine Hollow. He picked up the basket and returned to the front step. The man followed him and held the door until Ben returned for the groceries.

At that instant, Carole knew she would be seen. Her car was parked directly across from Ben's house. It was a car Ben knew well, since it was at Pine Hollow every day. It was too late to do anything about the situation she'd gotten herself into. She had to hope that he wouldn't look in her direction.

Ben stepped back out of the house and reached for the bags. As he stood up with them, his eyes lit on the car. For a second, Carole hoped he wouldn't see, wouldn't notice, wouldn't recognize, but their eyes met and her hopes were dashed. Ben had seen her; he knew she was there.

There were no nice words or rationalizations for what she was doing. She was spying on him. She was his friend, or had thought she was, and she was doing nothing more than snooping. No way could she pretend she'd just been wondering where Winn Road was. She was a nosy snoop. She knew it, and now Ben knew it.

Without a word or sign of acknowledgment, Ben stepped back into the house. The door closed behind him. A second later the welcome light went out.

NINE

It occurred to Carole to call in sick the next morning, but that seemed dishonest, and she'd had enough of her own dishonesty for a while. She arrived at Pine Hollow very early and was in the office and behind the desk by the time Max arrived.

She flicked on the computer and began her data input before the horses had been fed or the first stall had been mucked out. If she was busy working at the computer, she wouldn't be able to help with the physical chores, and that would, at least, put off the inevitable meeting with Ben, for his first task was always looking after the horses. She suspected he would be as happy to avoid her as she was to avoid him.

As she worked, Carole could hear the familiar sounds of the stable waking up: stalls being mucked out, hay coming down from the loft, fresh shavings being spread in the stalls. These soothing sounds helped her concentration, which was so total that she was almost finished entering the address file when the first class of young riders arrived, clamoring for their pony assignments.

By midmorning, Carole had convinced herself that if she sat at the desk for the rest of her life entering names and addresses, she could successfully avoid seeing the one person she never wanted to see. Then he appeared at the door to the office.

"Barq just threw a shoe," he said.

"I'll let the farrier know," Carole responded. "He'll be here Monday."

"Thanks."

That was it, their total conversation. No accusations, no recriminations. Carole returned to the computer, uncertain whether that was good or bad.

At eleven Emily arrived with Callie. Mrs. Forester had brought both of them and was staying to watch the session. Carole was surprised that there was going to be any session at all.

"It's really just a bruise," Callie said. "It only hurts a little, and although I don't mind sympathy, I hardly deserve any. Even my doctor said some exercise wouldn't hurt the new injury. So I'm doing the classic back-in-the-saddle thing."

Emily seemed pleased about the whole matter. Mrs. Forester looked skeptical. The trio left the office to get to work.

"At least let me carry the saddle," Mrs. Forester said to the two girls.

"Let you? We're going to shanghai you for the job. And how are you with a grooming bucket?" Emily asked, once again defusing a potentially explosive situation with humor. It was a gift Carole envied.

When Carole could no longer look at her computer screen, she decided to check on Callie and Emily, wondering how the pair was surmounting the problems of the newest handicap. She walked along the stable aisle to the schooling ring, automatically greeting horses as she went. Fez, in his Ben-made sling, barely acknowledged her as she passed by.

She reached the door that led to the ring and paused, remaining in the shadow of the stable. Callie was in the saddle, holding the reins in her good hand. Ben held a lead line and was walking next to PC's head. The greenest beginning rider always had a lead walker, and it must have been humiliating to Callie to have Ben there. The reality was that although PC was the finest and gentlest of horses, nobody wanted to take any chances, even Callie. Her balance was distorted from the accident, and her skills were further hampered by her bruised ankle. She was very much at risk. Riding was supposed to help her. Falling off a startled horse would not be helpful.

At Emily's instruction, Ben helped Callie take her feet out of the stirrups. PC began walking slowly. Carole could see Callie shift her weight through her hips to move with the motion of the walking horse. It was the most natural thing in the world for a healthy rider. For Callie, with damage to her nervous system, it was training. If her body had forgotten how to walk smoothly, PC was reminding her nerves and her brain just what it was she was supposed to do.

"Is your bruised ankle hurting?" Mrs. Forester asked from the fence.

"Not much, Mom. No problem."

"Emily? Does she mean that?" Mrs. Forester asked.

"Probably not," Emily said. "But it doesn't matter. Even though it may hurt a little, she's not doing anything that will cause further damage."

Emily was perched atop the fence so that she could see everything. She had a clipboard in her hand and was making notes and check marks while Callie rode smoothly and comfortably. Every few minutes Emily's concentration was broken by another worried query from Mrs. Forester. She wasn't worried about anything in particular. She was worried about everything—the speed at which Ben was walking the horse, the angle of the turns, the possibility that PC might be distracted by the jumping class in the adjacent ring.

Then Emily had another of her wonderful problem-solving ideas.

"Would you be able to take the lead rope for a while?" she asked. "I know Ben has some chores he wants to get to."

Mrs. Forester agreed readily. It was a good idea, and Carole knew it instantly. Mrs. Forester was a rider herself and was wise about horses. The problem with watching her daughter's therapy was that she didn't have any control. As soon as she became involved—leading the horse—she'd be a participant and could stop fretting about other people's, and horses', mistakes.

Mrs. Forester eagerly took the rope from Ben, who excused himself from the session. He would now come into the stable, probably to Fez's stall. Carole returned to the computer, hoping she could avoid seeing him and talking to him for a while longer—like a hundred years.

She worked at the computer, answered the phone, called the farrier. In the far distance she could just hear Emily, Callie, and Mrs. Forester in the ring. The rest of the therapeutic session went as smoothly as the first half had. Soon enough, Carole heard the clopping hooves as PC returned to the stable. If Ben had chores to do, the least she could do was untack PC, groom him, and bring him some water.

She met the group at his stall. Emily was running up his stirrups. Carole took over the job and removed the saddle, letting PC loose in his stall.

Callie and her mother were more interested in what was going on on the other side of the hall, in Fez's stall. Carole watched the interchange.

"What is that?" Mrs. Forester asked, looking at the sling.

Ben explained it to her while he loosened the straps. "He's been up long enough now. It's time for a rest."

Mrs. Forester asked Ben questions about the schedule, not in a challenging way, but clearly interested in what was being done for the welfare of her daughter's horse.

While her mother talked and listened, Callie watched. Carole could see that what held her attention wasn't the chatter, the comparison of her therapeutic riding with the therapeutic program Ben had devised for Fez. What Callie was watching was her horse. He might be standing. He might be stronger today than yesterday. But there was still no gleam in his eye, no interested perk to his ears. She reached out and patted his cheek. He barely responded; his eyes simply followed her hand. He took the carrot she offered him, but there was no grateful nod or eager sniff for a follow-up morsel.

Emily was laughing, looking at Ben's chart. "You know, I think the only real difference here between the program you've set up for Fez and the one I've got for Callie is that I don't have her scheduled for any longeing and pasture time—and longeing might not be a bad idea."

Callie stepped into the stall with Fez and Ben, using her crutches for support. Fez was still standing, though waiting for Ben to release the last few straps so that he could lie down. Callie leaned forward and reached down, feeling the leg that had been broken in the accident. It was much thinner than his other leg, weakened by the break and atrophied from lack of use.

"We've got some work to do, you and me," she told the horse. He watched her without moving his head, and then, when Ben unbuckled the final strap, Fez let himself down into the soft straw bedding, watching Callie until he lowered his head and closed his eyes.

"I think it's nap time for Fez," Mrs. Forester said cheerily. She held the stall door for Callie, saw that Ben wasn't finished there, and closed it behind her daughter. Emily followed Mrs. Forester and Callie down the hallway. They'd worked hard and deserved a rest.

For Carole there was the job of looking after PC. And across the hall, Ben worked with Fez, folding the sling, soothing the ailing horse, and making sure that the straw bed was soft and giving. They worked without speaking. For a while, Carole thought maybe it would be possible that they wouldn't speak, wouldn't have to consider what had gone on the night before.

When she finished grooming PC, it was time to get him a bucket of water and a tick of hay. She picked up the empty water bucket and the full grooming bucket and let herself into the aisle, latching the stall door behind her.

Ben was coming out of Fez's stall with his water bucket. There was no question about it. They were headed in the same direction, and neither of them could pretend they weren't staring at one another and that there wasn't something they needed to talk about.

"You get lost last night?" Ben asked, more as a challenge than a question.

At first, Carole didn't know how to answer.

"Wrong side of town," he said, reminding her of where she'd been.

"I—Uh . . . ," she stammered. This wasn't good. "I'm sorry, Ben. I guess I wanted to know—I mean, I knew the address and, well, I knew you were walking, so I thought maybe you'd want a ride home."

"Yeah, right," he said. "Look, if I'd wanted a ride home, I would have taken one when you offered it. And you weren't going to do me any good parked across the street from my house."

"Ben, I—"

"I don't think we need to talk about it, Carole. I thought we were friends. Friends respect one another."

"I'm sorry, Ben," Carole said.

"Okay," he said, accepting her apology as abruptly as it had been delivered.

With that, he touched his forehead in a small salute and walked past her to the tack room.

TEN

"'Okay'? All he said was 'Okay'?" Stevie asked.

Carole nodded glumly. "I think it was the stupidest thing I ever did."

"It wasn't bright," Stevie agreed.

"I was just curious."

"He's so private, though," Stevie said. "There has to be a reason."

"Well, I didn't learn much except that he lives in a kind of run-down house in a kind of run-down neighborhood with a man who looks like he's probably his grandfather."

"You don't know who else lives in the house," Stevie reminded her.

"No. I guess I don't. And I don't even know that the man is his grandfather. But I do know that Ben looks after him because he brought groceries and he took down the laundry."

"I wonder what the secret is," Stevie mused. "Don't you?"

"The secret is probably that he doesn't like being spied on by someone he thought was a friend. It doesn't matter what I learned or didn't learn, I hurt his feelings."

"He accepted your apology," Stevie said.

"Sure. Like he meant it, too."

Carole and Stevie were sitting on the floor in Stevie's room, where they'd had many conferences over the years. As soon as Carole had left Pine Hollow that evening, she'd walked over to Stevie's, wanting the solace of a friend. She'd gotten dinner along with the solace, and now they were having the private chat she'd needed all day.

Carole grasped her knees and pulled them tight to her chest.

"You don't do a lot of stupid things," Stevie said. It didn't sound like a compliment, and it wasn't really meant as one. Carole recognized it as a simple truthful statement. She didn't do stupid things.

"On the other hand," Stevie continued, "I'm famous for them. I've been accused of impulsive behavior more times than I care to recall. I regret it every time, especially when it hurts someone I didn't mean to hurt. All I can tell you, Carole, is that it passes. Ben will forget. So will you. I have to say I don't think this is a very good way to begin a relationship—"

"There *is* no relationship," Carole interrupted.

Stevie withdrew the assertion with a quick "Right," and then said, "No matter. But the only thing to do is to forget it."

"I can't."

"Well, then, pretend to forget it, because that's what Ben will do."

Carole sighed. In this case, Stevie probably knew what she was talking about. Carole wasn't very good at pretending and she never had been. This, perhaps, would be an appropriate time to start honing the skill.

"You know, I've been thinking about that postcard from Lisa, and every time I think about it, I miss her a little bit more. Want to see if we can get her on the phone?" Stevie asked.

"That's a wonderful idea," Carole said. "What time is it out there?"

"Oh, about"—Stevie looked at her watch—"six. She ought to be home from work. Probably helping Evelyn with dinner or something like that. Want to try?"

"Hand me the phone," Carole said.

Stevie took the cordless phone from her bedside table and punched Talk. She listened for the dial tone, but instead heard voices. She covered the phone with her hand and listened tentatively for a few seconds.

". . . mucking out stables, just stuff like that—I hardly see Skye at all," a very familiar voice said.

Stevie pointed to the phone and mouthed "Lisa" to Carole. "And Alex." Then she spoke. "Uh, yeah, I'm here. . . . No, I'm not listening in. I just wanted to use the phone to call a friend in California. Hi, Lis'! . . . Listen, Carole's here and we're dying to catch up, so when my darling twin finishes telling you how miserable he's making everybody in the family because he misses you so much, have him come get me so Carole and I can give you details. And Alex, bring your phone in here so we can each have one, please. . . . Okay, okay, I'm hanging up now."

She poked Talk again, leaving her brother and his girlfriend alone.

Over the next fifteen minutes, Stevie lightened Carole's mood by sharing tales from the laundry. Only Stevie could have found a way to make color-bleeding funny or make a riveting story out of a malfunctioning extractor. Flows of suds, disputes over socks, and abandoned sweatshirts all combined into interesting events.

In the middle of a story about a couple who found an unfamiliar set of women's underwear among their laundry, Alex knocked on the door and handed Carole his cordless phone.

"She's all yours, for now," he said.

Stevie reached for her phone so that she and Carole could talk at once. "How *are* you?" she began.

Lisa was fine, it seemed. Everything she'd said in the postcard was true, though, naturally, there was a good deal more to tell.

Her job at the television ranch was really great. "They have these wonderful horses here. They are so well trained and their owners demand contracts so that the horses get total star treatment."

"*Yadda yadda* on the horses," Stevie interrupted—although Carole would have liked to hear more about their special care. "Tell us about the human stars, starting with Skye Ransom."

Lisa told them. She didn't see an awful lot of Skye, and when she did see him, he was usually dashing from one place to another, stopping by only to pick up or drop off his horse. He was the star of the television series, but there were other stars, too, some nice, some not so nice. Lisa didn't spend much time with any of them, either. She wasn't complaining. They were paying her well, and it was really interesting, for a summer job. Then Lisa turned the tables and started asking questions.

She knew all about the accident and Callie's

recovery. She even knew that Callie was using riding as therapy. Carole and Stevie brought her up to date on the first few sessions, including the bruised ankle.

"Oh no!" said Lisa.

"She's being a great sport about it," Carole said. "She's even almost convinced us that it's not a bad thing. It makes her disabled on both sides, not just one, so it evens things up for her."

"Only Callie would find a silver lining in that particular cloud," Lisa said. "And how's everybody else—Max, Red, Ben, like that?"

"Fine," said Carole.

"Ahem," said Stevie.

"Mostly fine," Carole said.

"A-*hem*!" Stevie said more pointedly.

"Well, there is this little problem," Carole said, and she told Lisa what had happened. "I feel really stupid," she concluded.

"Stevie's right," Lisa told her. "You have to ignore it. You don't have another choice."

Somehow, when Lisa said it, it made more sense than when Stevie had said it. Perhaps hearing it from someone coolly logical rather than infamously illogical made the idea more palatable and sensible.

"Thanks, Lis'," Carole said. "I'll try."

"Um, I've got to go give Evelyn a hand with dinner now," Lisa said.

"We didn't even get to ask you about your dad, Evelyn, and Lily," said Stevie.

"They're all fine. Lily is crawling, nearly walking. She's a little devil, and she's cute as can be. Dad and Evelyn are doing great, especially now that Lily is sleeping through the night. They send love."

"Us, too," said Carole.

"We'll talk again soon," said Stevie.

"Definitely," said Lisa. "Bye." And she hung up.

Stevie and Carole hung up as well. A few seconds later Alex appeared to retrieve his phone. Carole handed it to him, thanking him for the loan.

"She sounds great," Stevie said brightly.

"Do you think she's having too much fun?" Alex asked.

"Give yourself a break," Carole advised. "She's having a good summer, and that's good news. Would you rather that she were miserable?"

Alex chewed that thought for a few seconds and then shook his head. "No, I guess not."

"How many times have I told you that Lisa and Skye are just good friends?" said Stevie.

"About a million," he said.

"So, make this a million and one."

"Thanks." He backed out the room, closing the door behind him.

"She *is* having fun," said Stevie.

"Maybe she won't come home," Carole said. The thought was not comforting. "Speaking of which, I think it's time for me to go." She stood up and stretched, a little stiff from sitting on the floor. "Thanks for dinner; thanks for listening; thanks for the call to Lisa," she said.

"You are more than welcome," Stevie told her. "Mom always says I'm supposed to invite you to dinner anytime."

"Well, I'm glad you invited me tonight," Carole said, hugging her friend.

The two of them walked to the front door. As they passed the den, Carole said good night and thanked Stevie's parents.

"Good night, Carole," said Mr. Lake. "Do you need a lift someplace?"

"Oh, no, thank you. I needed to work out some kinks so I walked over from Pine Hollow, but my car's there. I'm going to pick it up now. Good night, and again, thanks."

"I'll talk to you soon," said Stevie.

Carole waved a final good-bye and set out in the moonlit night to Pine Hollow.

ELEVEN

Usually by ten o'clock at night, Pine Hollow was completely dark, the horses were settled down, and all the lights were off in the Regnery house, which was next door to the stable. As Carole approached that night, though, there was a light in the office, and she could see a few lights in the stable. The first thought that occurred to her was that it was her fault, that she'd left lights on, probably left the computer running, was guilty of leaving lights on all through the stable. On reflection, that was out of the question. When she'd left at five-thirty, it had still been daylight and few lights, if any, would have been on in the stable. Moreover, there had been lots of people still around, many of whom might have turned on lights. The more logical conclusion was that someone was still there.

She let herself into the stable through the office door. Her computer was turned off and snugly protected by its dust cover, as she'd left it. She dropped her backpack on the office chair and headed into the stable to see if anyone was there.

The horses were quiet, ready for darkness and sleep. They barely noticed her as she walked through. It didn't take long to find the source of the light. Just two hall lights and a stall light were on, and they were all at Fez's stall. Carole looked over the door to find that Ben was taking care of Fez.

The horse was lying down on his side. He was thrashing his legs, clearly in discomfort. Ben was next to him, talking quietly in that tone he used that only horses seemed to understand. He glanced up and saw Carole.

"Can you use a hand?" she asked, letting herself into the stall.

"I think he could," Ben answered.

"You gave him something for the pain?"

"I just did, but it hasn't taken hold yet. I thought I'd sit with him until he calmed down."

Ben held the horse's sore leg in his hands and massaged it ever so gently. Fez made no effort to pull the leg from Ben's touch, so it was reasonable for Ben to think that whatever he was doing was comforting to Fez. He kept on doing it and continued with what Carole thought of as his sweet talk.

Carole sat down in the straw. She lifted the horse's head and slid her legs under it, becoming the horse's pillow. She stroked his cheek and his nose, his forehead and his neck, smoothly and softly.

Carole watched Ben at work, gentle and kind. The veins stood out on his strong hands, and his brow furrowed in concentration. He crouched, ready to move if Fez should threaten him with the now decreasing thrashes of his limbs. It was hard for Carole to fit together the sullen and private Ben who'd chastised her so that afternoon with the Ben who now gave his rapt attention to the ailing horse. How could someone with so much love for horses be so distant with people? It occurred to her at that moment that perhaps it was people and not horses who had hurt him in the past. Carole kept the thought to herself and went on patting Fez softly.

Fez's dark eyes shifted ever so slightly to look at her and then closed. Fez accepted her kindness along with Ben's. She could feel the full weight of his head on her lap as he relaxed.

It was a quiet moment in the stable. There was the occasional contented sound of the horses nearby, a snort, the clop of a hoof shifting position. Outside she could hear crickets chirping. In the stall she heard the slow, even breathing of the horse, whose pain was subsiding, and she heard Ben's gentle massage and his soft, sweet talk. Fez's thrashing slowed even more. He took a deep breath, sighed, and slept painlessly.

Neither Carole nor Ben spoke or moved for a long time. Ben gradually stopped his massage, then slipped his hands under Fez's cheek and supported his head so that Carole could slide out from under its weight. She piled some straw where she'd been sitting to make a pillow and watched as Ben lowered the resting horse's head onto the straw. The medicine had taken hold; Fez would sleep now, long and hard.

The two caretakers crept out of the stall on tiptoe, like the parents of a sick child. Ben switched off the light that had illuminated the stall; Carole clicked off the overheads. They tiptoed down the stable aisle and went into the office, pulling the door closed behind them.

Ben spoke first. "You're really good with horses," he said.

"You too," she answered.

"You care, don't you?"

"A lot. More than most people understand."

"It's the same for me," Ben told her. "Horses have always been what's good in my life."

That was something Carole could understand. What she wasn't so sure about was why Ben was saying this to her.

"Working with them is how I stay near that good. The way I can work the most is if I get the training I need. That's why I'm applying for that grant for a preveterinary degree from the Horsemen's Association. In order to get the grant, I have to do a project. That's what Fez's therapy program is all about. But don't get me wrong. I mean, I like the horse okay—even though he wasn't all that nice to me, or to you for that matter, when he was healthy—but if he makes it, it'll prove that I know what I'm doing with horses. I made the plan for the program myself, but I got approval from both Max and Judy before I did anything with the horse. Judy even showed it to the specialist who worked with Fez at the clinic.

"Never mind that they approved it; none of them thinks it's going to work. They say the Foresters should have let Judy euthanize Fez right after the accident. Maybe they're right. Maybe they're right that it won't work, but I have to try. That grant is the only hope I have for going to college. Fez has to get better. He just has to."

Carole was stunned. She had no idea what to say to Ben and, for once, realized that perhaps saying nothing was the best thing she could do. She nodded while she considered what had just happened.

In a way, what he said didn't surprise her. She'd pretty much figured out that he was applying for a grant and that Fez's program was an integral part of the application. The stunning part was that he'd told her about it and that he'd told her in such a personal way. Ben Marlow had totally opened up to her on one—just one—very important subject.

Fez's survival and Ben's were tied together. If Fez made it despite the gloomy speculations of Judy, Max, and the specialist, then it would prove to anyone who had any sense that Ben Marlow knew what he was doing with horses. Of course, anybody who had ever seen Ben lead a horse into its stall knew that he had a special touch with horses. If the Horsemen's Association needed more proof than that, Ben would provide it, and Carole would help him. Since he'd opened up to her, she could do so with him.

"I'd like to help you," she said.

"You have," he answered.

"And I will again."

"Okay," he said.

Ben reached to turn out the ceiling light in the office while Carole clicked off the one on the desk. He followed her through the door to the outside and pulled it shut behind him, locking it and stowing the key.

Carole fetched her car keys from her handbag.

"Can I give you a lift?" she asked, almost automatically.

"No thanks, Carole," he said stiffly. He shoved his hands into his pockets and walked down the driveway and onto the street without turning back or saying good night.

Some healing had taken place, Carole knew, but it was clear that wounds remained and that there were places she was still not invited to go—his home among them.

TWELVE

There was a pleasant feeling of normalcy around Pine Hollow the next morning. Carole worked industriously at the computer, stopping occasionally to answer the phone, switch horse and pony assignments, or solve a problem.

By midmorning, she'd made a list of horses for the farrier to check on Monday, she'd set up another computer file, she'd answered half an hour's worth of questions from a potential boarder, and she'd successfully avoided any further conversations with Ben Marlow. *A morning well spent,* she teased herself.

Callie and Emily were working together again that morning. Carole had helped them by carrying PC's tack to his stall and had then stopped to check on Fez, who did not seem one iota better. Nor did he seem any worse, and that had to be considered good news.

Carole could hear them working together

outside her window. Denise McCaskill was helping them as well, taking the lead rope. Now that Mrs. Forester had satisfied herself that it really was safe and that the people at Pine Hollow—including her daughter—knew what they were doing, she was off the hook as general supervisor of all things therapeutic and was spending the morning at the beauty parlor.

The sounds from Pine Hollow's mini–therapeutic riding center were positively giddy, even if it was clear that they didn't mean a lot of progress was being made.

"Hey, this is neat," said Callie. "You've trained this old boy to verbal commands, haven't you? I can just say 'left' or 'right' and he does it without any other aids."

"Yep," Emily said. "And if we were working to strengthen your vocal cords, that would be a good exercise for you. But . . ."

Callie laughed. It was a happy and relaxed sound. "Left . . . Right . . . Left . . . Right," she intoned.

"You're making me dizzy!" Denise complained.

"*Straight,*" commanded Callie. "There, is that better?"

"Much, unless that includes walking into the fence."

"I think I know what PC stands for," said Callie. "Perfectly Compliant?"

"No, I think it's Probably Crazy," Denise offered. Emily, who claimed to have named her horse, also claimed that either she didn't know what PC stood for or that whatever it stood for changed frequently.

"Nope, you're both wrong. For now it's Properly Chastised, which is what he deserves to be for dumping you the other day."

"He didn't mean to," Callie said. "I'm sure it was my fault, and it doesn't matter anyway because it's hardly a problem at all. Now, go left, PC, left."

"Use your leg as much as you can," said Emily. "Good. That's right—I mean correct."

It pleased Carole to hear the light and happy chatter while they worked. They might be joking, but she knew they were also working hard. Hard work could be fun, especially when it had to do with horses.

Ben was showing the beginner class how to groom a pony. Under Max's instruction, he was introducing them to currycombs, dandy brushes, hoof picks, rags, and sponges. It was a complicated business for the beginners, and teaching them was a lot of work.

The phone rang again, and Carole turned her attention back to the job at hand.

"Pine Hollow," she said, answering the call.

"It's me."

"Hello, Stevie," Carole said. "How's the laundry business?"

"It's slow today. The boss said I could have the rest of the day off if I wanted to, and I want to. I was thinking that you'll only be working for a little while longer, and then we might do some ring work with the horses. Does that sound like a good idea to you?"

"Excellent," Carole said. "Brilliant, inspired, and simply good as well. What time can you get here?"

"Well, I was sort of thinking you might perhaps want to come pick me up?"

"I would?"

"Almost certainly," Stevie said.

"Why not?" Carole agreed. "I'll be there in about half an hour. You've got riding clothes here?"

"Yes, and boots as well."

"See you then," Carole said, cradling the phone.

The laundry was at the nearby shopping center, less than a mile from Pine Hollow. The girls had walked the route together hundreds of times because their favorite hangout—the ice cream parlor, TD's—was at the same shopping center. It was a little unusual for Stevie to ask for a ride, but if she needed help, Carole was going to give it to her. After all, it was only last night that Stevie had spent a fair amount of time trying to help her with the mess she'd gotten herself into with Ben. Besides, if Carole drove Stevie over to Pine Hollow, they could start riding sooner.

Carole tidied up her desk, turning off the computer and straightening out the papers and pencils for Denise.

There were twenty minutes left in Carole's shift, but nothing said she had to spend them all at the desk. She decided to devote the time to tacking up Belle and Starlight.

Starlight's nostrils flared eagerly when Carole approached with his saddle. He knew it was almost time for them to have a ride, and he seemed eager to get going. He stood absolutely still while she put on his saddle and bridle. Belle was every bit as cooperative, though she seemed a little curious as to why the job was being done by Carole instead of Stevie. Carole glanced at her watch as she secured Belle's saddle. It was noon, and that meant the end of her workday.

She latched Belle's stall door behind her and went to tell Denise she was leaving. She also told Callie and Emily that she and Stevie were going to ride for a while and asked if they'd like to join them.

"You're done with your work for the day, aren't you?"

"We sure are," Emily said.

"Then how about some play?"

"Sounds good to me," Emily told her.

"Me too," Callie agreed. "I guess. I mean, as long as we don't do anything too . . . well . . ."

"Don't worry," Carole said. "We won't do barrel racing until *next* week."

"Deal," said Callie.

"I'll be back with Stevie in ten minutes," Carole promised.

She fished her car keys out of her bag and left for the shopping center.

Stevie was waiting for her in front of the laundry. Carole reached across the passenger seat and opened the door for her. Stevie had to be feeling pretty low to have asked for a lift from the shopping center to Pine Hollow. There was no point in asking her about that.

"This is the complete chauffeur service," Carole announced, welcoming Stevie to the car. "Belle and Starlight are both tacked up and waiting, and I've invited Callie and Emily to ride with us."

Stevie settled into the seat and smiled contentedly. "Thank you, Carole. I knew you'd understand."

Carole did, of course. The night before had mostly been spent on her and the dumb thing she'd done to Ben. That couldn't make her forget the fact that Stevie had been very low recently. Carole was glad to help her.

Nobody who had been in the car that rainy afternoon would ever be able to forget the horror of the accident, the scream of the horse, the terrifying rolling that never seemed to stop. The lasting effects of the accident were very different for all of them, but they were there. Carole's scratches had healed quickly; Stevie's broken ribs still bothered her sometimes, but they were almost all better; nobody knew how long Callie's residual brain damage would remain or if it would ever go away. What would never go away for any of them, though, was the memories. Sometimes Carole would wake up in the night, still feeling the car tumbling down the hill, feeling her shoulder jolting against the door repeatedly, feeling her body straining against her seat belt, slamming into Stevie next to her. She knew Stevie shared these nightmares. It was the last time she'd driven. Carole wondered when she'd be ready to drive again. The new car Stevie shared with Alex was sitting in the driveway of the Lakes' house because Alex was spending his summer days on a lawn crew that drove around town on a truck large enough to hold its equipment. The car was Stevie's all day, every day. She just wasn't ready to drive.

She was, however, ready to ride. As soon as Carole stopped the car at Pine Hollow, Stevie jumped out, eager to be with Belle. It only took her a few minutes to change her clothes. Stevie and Carole tightened their horses' girths, mounted up, touched the good-luck horseshoe, and rode out into the ring.

While Carole had been gone, Emily had tacked up Patch for herself. Patch didn't have the specialty training PC did, but he was gentle and reliable.

"Are you tired yet?" Carole asked Callie.

"Not a bit," Callie said with certainty. "Remember, my specialty is endurance riding."

Carole smiled. "This isn't exactly the same thing," she said.

"No, but it involves long hours in the saddle. I've just been here for about forty-five minutes and I don't think we've gone faster than a walk, have we, PC?"

Emily answered for her horse. "No, we haven't, and we won't. You're not ready for anything more than a walk yet. I checked my charts and they don't say trot for another three pages."

"And canter?"

"I don't read that far ahead," said Emily.

"Besides, walking is a nice gait—one of my favorites. You can do a lot of things at a walk."

"Name one," said Callie.

Carole glanced up at the sky. It was a beautiful sunny day, no clouds and bright sunshine. Just as she'd hoped. "Shadow tag," she said. "You're It!" With that, she moved Starlight over to the shadow cast by Belle and Stevie.

"You always make me It first!" Stevie complained, shifting Belle to her right. "Why don't you make someone like Emily be It?" With that, Stevie reached over to Emily's shadow.

"Me?" Emily said, kicking Patch gently and getting him to walk toward Callie on PC. "Why me? Why not someone like . . ." She stretched her arm until her own shadow merged with Callie's.

Callie, now It, used her weakened legs to get PC moving at a walk. She headed straight for Stevie, who managed to evade the shadow by backing up. Then, while Stevie was still out of reach, Callie uttered the simple command, "Left, PC." PC immediately turned left, leaving Callie within shadow-touching distance of Carole. "You're It!" she said.

"Sneak! You're a sneak!" Carole said, more pleased than she could say at the way Callie had fooled them.

Carole couldn't remember the last time she'd

played shadow tag. It was a favorite of the young riders at Pine Hollow, and she'd played it in many classes and Pony Club meetings, but not for a long time and never at a walk. She now found herself wondering why it had been so long. The four of them were having a terrific time playing in the sunshine.

By the third round of "Its," Callie was obviously tiring, and Patch, though well trained, was clearly a little difficult for Emily. Carole declared Callie the winner. Callie objected, saying she'd had an unfair advantage because she was riding PC. Nobody disputed that. Nor did they dispute Carole's assertion that it was time for Callie to call it a day—as long as the losers had the right to call a rematch at a future date. Callie said she'd be only too happy to show them some of the other fine points of shadow tag at a walk. "If you can wait two or three pages, as Emily puts it, we might even move this up to a trot!"

The deal was made.

Ben, finished with his grooming demonstration, came into the small schooling ring and offered to look after PC for Callie.

"No, I can groom him," she said. "But I'll let you do the hard part."

"Which is . . . ?"

"Carrying tack and bringing water," she told him.

"Whatever you say." He took PC's lead, and Callie rode back into the stable on the horse.

Carole and Stevie began trotting around the ring. Stevie brought Belle up next to Starlight so that they could talk while they rode.

"A penny for your thoughts," she said to Carole, who was deep in concentration.

"I was thinking about handicaps," Carole said.

"Like Callie's?" Stevie asked her.

"More like the general nature of handicaps," Carole told her. "The other day I was talking with Emily about the difference between Callie's temporary disability and her permanent one. She said she'd be nuts if she didn't wish she was normal. That got me thinking about what normal is and what a handicap is. I mean, look at someone like Ben. Never mind that what I did was awful—it was and we don't need to go over it again. If Ben were more, um, normal, I wouldn't have been tempted. If he didn't insist on being so secretive about himself, I wouldn't be curious."

"Carole, it's not like he's trying to be secretive—"

"No, but it *is* like he can't ask for help. One of the things that makes Emily so special is that she asks for help—when she needs it. Callie does the same thing. Ben doesn't know how. I think that's a kind of handicap, too. You can't give it crutches or a wheelchair or physical therapy, but it's a handicap."

"Hmmm," Stevie said. There was a long pause. "So, what about . . ."

Before Stevie could phrase her question, Scott Forester walked into the ring. He waved at the two girls, and they drew their horses to a walk and went over to him.

"Carole, I just wanted to remind you about the party tomorrow. You too," he said to Stevie quickly. "And Phil as well. We'll be starting about five o'clock, snacks, dinner, swimming, a real down-home barbecue. I hope you'll be there."

"We wouldn't miss it for anything," Carole assured him.

"See you," he said, waving good-bye to both of them.

The horses picked up their trot again.

"What were you about to ask?" Carole asked.

Stevie shook her head. "I forget," she said.

THIRTEEN

On Saturday morning, Carole came to Pine Hollow with an extra backpack to hold her party gear—a clean set of clothes and a bathing suit. She'd have to shower before she went over to the Foresters', because she'd discovered over the years that not everybody in the world loved the scent of horses and barns quite as much as she did.

Pine Hollow was always busy on Saturdays, especially on summer Saturdays. There was no Pony Club meeting this morning, and Carole had agreed to work at the desk. There was no time to think about anything—parties, handicaps, injuries, or therapy. It was a refreshing change. The only thing Carole had decided for sure was that it was important for Ben to go to the Foresters'. He'd been invited, and he should be there. She could imagine how hard he would protest. He could probably think of a hundred reasons not to be around the smooth and worldly Scott Forester. She wanted to see to it that Ben didn't have anything to protest about, so the one thing she'd decided, aside from a shower, was that the last thing she'd do before she left would be to check in on Fez—where she was sure to find Ben—to try to convince him to come.

In spite of her intentions to focus totally on the pile of work in front of her, she found herself debating with the imaginary Ben all morning long.

"Why should you feel uncomfortable around Scott? Surely it isn't because he's rich and the son of a famous politician. I'm not rich, and I'm not the daughter of a famous politician, and I'm not uncomfortable around Scott. Quite the contrary. He's always nice to me . . ."

No, that wouldn't do. Whatever went on in Ben's mind, the fact that Scott flirted mercilessly with every girl didn't seem to be a strong talking point to lure Ben to the party. Scott's flirtatious manner clearly irritated Ben. Then how about this?

"The Foresters have planned this lovely party to say thank you to all of us who have helped Callie, and you've been enormously helpful to her."

Yes, that seemed like a better tack.

"Carole?"

She looked up, surprised to find a woman standing next to her, holding a check.

"I'm sorry, my mind was someplace else." Carole blushed, accepting the check. She decided she really didn't have time to argue with Ben.

At three-thirty, Carole relinquished the desk to Denise, who by then was eager for an opportunity to sit down. Carole took her bag, dropped it off in the locker area, and headed for Fez's stall.

As expected, she found Ben there. What she didn't expect, however, was to see Fez lying down. She'd checked his chart. He was supposed to be in his sling for an hour now. Carole had thought she'd be able to help groom him.

Ben was next to him, tensely crouched, much as he had been the other night when Fez had been thrashing so uncomfortably.

"What's the problem?" Carole asked.

Ben shook his head. "I can't get him to stand," he said. "He's so well trained that usually a good tug at his lead rope gets him standing for me, even when he really doesn't want to."

Carole let herself into the stall. "Sometimes it's psychological, you know."

"How's that?"

"Well, look. Did you ever try to lead a horse by looking back at him?"

"Sure, and it doesn't work. If he sees you stopped and staring at him, he'll stare back at you. It's probably some sort of passive confrontation thing with horses. You have to look straight ahead and walk straight ahead and he'll follow. But you can't stare him down."

"Right," Carole said. "And now maybe it's sort of like that. You can't convince him to stand up when you're crouched over him."

"Oh," said Ben. "Well, it's worth a try."

Ben stood up. He took the horse's lead rope and tugged. He didn't look into Fez's eyes, he looked at the sling, now waiting above the horse. Fez didn't move.

"Try again," Carole said, regarding Fez carefully. "He seems a little interested."

Ben tugged at the rope without looking at Fez. Slowly the horse shifted his weight and struggled to get his uncooperative legs under him. It took more than a few seconds, but then he was standing. As soon as that happened, Ben and Carole worked swiftly to get the sling around his belly to support him.

"I told you you were good with horses," Ben said.

"Lucky guess."

"More than that, and I'm glad you came by."

"Well, it isn't what I came by for," Carole said. "I came by to remind you about the Foresters' party and to offer you a ride over there."

"Okay," Ben said. "What time?"

"Five?"

"Sure," he agreed.

That was easy. Carole smiled, trying to recount to herself all the arguments she had prepared to make to him.

"What are you smiling about?" Ben challenged. Carole wished he weren't so observant.

"Oh, I don't know," she said evasively. "I guess I just thought you'd try to find a way to wriggle out of this party. You didn't seem too enthusiastic about it before."

"Well, I don't know that I'm exactly enthusiastic," Ben said. "I could probably do without an evening around Scott Forester, but I decided long ago that when a congressman tells me to do something, I'm going to do it."

It was that simple, after all.

When they had fastened the last of the straps, Ben and Carole checked Fez over carefully. Neither of them was happy with what they were seeing. If Fez had seemed listless before, it was even more apparent now. He'd stood up because he had been trained to be obedient. Carole brushed his coat and patted him while Ben checked his vital signs.

"He's got a low-grade fever," Ben said, looking up from the thermometer. "His pulse is a little elevated. I've got to make sure Max keeps an eye on him while we're gone."

"He's probably just tired from the effort to stand up," Carole said, hoping there was some truth to that.

"Maybe. Or maybe there's an infection. I'll check his temperature again before we go. We can take him out of the harness then, too."

"I know you're in charge, Ben, but considering how unhappy he looks right now, I think we'd be doing him a favor if we let him lie down. When he's feeling better tomorrow, you can have him in the sling for an extra-long stay."

Ben looked at the horse and shook his head. "That's two for you today, Carole," he said, reaching to loosen the first strap.

A few minutes later, Fez looked relieved to be lying back down in the straw. Carole headed for the shower in Max's house, and Ben went in search of Max to let him know what was going on with Fez.

Carole and Ben knew almost everybody at the party. The Foresters hadn't lived in Willow Creek very long, so the only people Callie knew were from Pine Hollow and the hospital. Her parents had a few friends there, including another congressman from near Callie's father's district. Stevie and Phil were there, as were Emily and Scott and a few other riders from Pine Hollow. Callie was sitting in a lounge chair by the pool, wearing a lacy cover-up over her bathing suit.

Most of the guests had suits and towels in their bags, and Mrs. Forester led them to bedrooms and bathrooms where they could change their clothes. Carole slipped into her suit and put her shirt back on over it. Stevie did the same.

Phil and Ben were already in the pool when Carole and Stevie came out of the house. Emily lowered herself into a lounge chair next to Callie's, piling her crutches on top of her friend's.

"Are we just going to watch?" Callie asked her therapeutic riding instructor.

"Up to you," Emily said.

"Let's go."

The two of them stood up together and, with a hand from Ben and Scott, made it to the pool's edge. Mrs. Forester saw what was happening from where she stood near the food table. She took a step, ready to intervene. Her husband, standing nearby, caught hold of her arm and held her. She looked at him, questioning. He simply nodded. She stood still.

Carole watched, fascinated, aware of Mrs. Forester's concern and equally aware of what was happening at the lip of the pool. As the two girls slid into the water, everything that hampered them on dry land slipped away. Each floated easily in the water. Callie stretched her arms in front of herself and swept them back, moving toward her brother. Emily followed her. Water, like horses, was an equalizer. The girls could do everything anybody else could when they were in the water.

Callie neared her brother. He reached out to her, offering his hands in support, which she did not accept. Instead, she moved her right arm back and then swept it forward in a rush, forcing a substantial wall of water right into his face.

"Splash fight!" she declared.

Carole and Stevie shed their shirts and jumped into the pool. Ben tossed a Frisbee to Emily, who used it to excellent effect on Phil, until Stevie's additional attack on him made him duck underwater and come up under her, tossing her three feet into the air. Stevie landed with a big splash that even reached some of the adults.

Emily's next rush of Frisbee-assisted water got everybody wet, including the dog, who decided at that point that *in* the pool was better than *out*. He turned out to be as effective a splasher as both of his owners, who by then were mastering the forward push of water, alternating with the sideswipe.

Carole took a deep breath, ducked under the water, and swam to the deep end of the pool, far from the splashers. She pulled herself out next to the diving board. From there she could watch.

Enormous energy was being expended at the other end of the pool. Almost every person there, including Carole, had been filled with anxiety about at least one thing recently. They'd been working hard, trying to help themselves and one another. They needed a way to let all the tension out. Carole was no exception.

She stood up and stepped onto the diving board. Starting at the far end, she ran as fast as she could. At the tip of the board she paused, bounced, rose high into the air, and then folded herself into as tight a ball as she could make. She landed in one of the most successful and spectacular cannonballs she'd ever made. If any of the adults had remained dry until then, they were not dry afterward.

When Carole came to the top, she found her friends applauding her feat. Then everybody had to try it, and it turned into a contest. It was hard for Callie and Emily because they had to have someone hold their hands as they made

144

their way along the diving board, and it was very hard for Emily to make a tight ball, but it wasn't hard for them to have fun doing it.

Ben was voted the overall winner, though everybody agreed that Carole's plunge had real style.

"I practice for hours every day," she said humbly into a pretend microphone that was really a barbecued rib. She took a bite out of it. It was delicious, sweet and tangy. She wondered briefly why anyone would have thought chicken might be a better idea than these ribs—until she tried the chicken, which was just as good. And Mrs. Forester's potato salad was special as well. Carole munched on some of the celery and carrot sticks between helpings of barbecue, hoping in vain that they might make up for all the good but fattening things she was otherwise consuming.

Nobody heard the phone ring except Congressman Forester, who was in the house getting more ice out of the freezer. He stepped out of the house and into the yard, casting his eye across the group of teenagers. "Ben?" he asked.

"Yes, sir?" Ben said, standing up and putting down his plate.

"The phone's for you. It's Max," Congressman Forester said.

Ben went pale. It couldn't be good news, and

everybody knew it. Carole went with Ben to answer the phone.

"Yes. . . . Right. . . . That's what I was afraid of. Judy said it might happen. . . . Right. . . . Okay, I'll be there." He hung up the phone.

"It's Fez," Ben sad. "He's not doing well at all. Max said he's thrashing around—"

"Just like the other night."

"Right, but medication hasn't calmed him at all."

"We've got to go."

"You don't have to—"

"Of course I do," Carole said.

"What's up?" Stevie asked, seeing Carole's and Ben's serious faces when she and Phil came into the house.

Carole told them.

"We'll come, too," said Phil.

"You don't have to," Ben said.

"Of course we do," said Stevie, echoing Carole.

Ben agreed. The four of them pulled their clothes on over their bathing suits and made their excuses to the Foresters and Emily, explaining what was going on.

Callie and Emily would want to be there as much as the other four, but there would be little they could do. They'd be better off staying home for the moment.

"Call us," Callie said.

"We will," Phil told her.

"Um, save some of that barbecue, will you?" Stevie asked.

"It's a deal," said Mrs. Forester.

Carole got her keys and had her engine going before all four doors were closed. Fez needed them. There was no time to waste.

FOURTEEN
14

It was worse. Carole expected to see Fez in the same condition she and Ben had found him in two nights before when they'd calmed him to sleep, but this was much worse. Fez's legs were flailing around purposelessly and painfully. His eyes, previously listless, were now open wide with fear.

"He's going to hurt himself," Max said. "We can't let him lie there."

"He was too tired to stand earlier."

"Well, he's too tired to lie down now," said Max. "Let's get him up. There are enough of us; we ought to be able to lift him, and then we can put him in his sling. Ben, Phil, get on that side. Carole, you stand over here with me. Stevie—um—"

"I know," Stevie said. "I should call Judy."

"Yes. Call Judy," Ben said, confirming what they all knew. Fez wasn't making it, and they needed Judy there to help.

Ben took over then, trying to use Carole's theory, the one that had worked earlier. It wasn't working now. They really would have to lift the horse, and they were probably going to have to use the sling to do it.

Stevie fled. She couldn't stand to watch. She knew a dying horse when she saw one. Fez was in great pain, and he'd been allowed to heal long enough that if he wasn't well now, he wasn't going to be. Everybody there knew that. They needed Judy, and they needed her as soon as possible.

Stevie reached the phone in the office and dialed the very familiar number of Pine Hollow's equine veterinarian. Judy wasn't there.

"Do you know where she is?" Stevie asked Judy's husband, Alan.

"A horse farm called Paget's Pride. It's a ways from here. The man has a mare that's going to foal soon—"

"Can you call her cell phone?"

"Battery's dead," Alan said. "I tried earlier and there was no answer, or maybe she left it in the truck. Then I called the farmhouse but got the answering machine. I'm sure she'll be back by morning."

Morning would be too late. It would mean another twelve hours of pain for the suffering horse. Fez was a valuable horse; insurance and other legal considerations had to be weighed in making a decision. They needed a veterinarian there, and on a Saturday night there was no way they could get anybody but Judy. Now they couldn't get Judy, either.

"Paget's Pride?" Stevie asked. "Isn't that on River Road?"

"That's the one," said Alan.

Stevie knew it. It was on a road she'd taken many times on the way to Phil's house. It was perhaps half an hour away; then it would take some time to find Judy and the owner with the mare in foal, and another half hour to come back. The soonest Judy could be at Pine Hollow would be an hour and a half, but that was a lot sooner than the next morning.

"Thanks," Stevie said. "I'll go over there. If you hear from her, let her know we've got an emergency here at Pine Hollow."

"Fez?" Alan asked.

"Yes, Fez," Stevie said.

"She was afraid of that."

"We all were."

She hung up and hurried back to the stall, where she saw the foursome struggling to get Fez on his feet.

"Judy's over at a farm on River Road and she's not near her phone. I'll go get her. Carole, I'll take your car."

150

At that moment Carole's hands were occupied with supporting and patting Fez's head.

"Right-hand pocket," she said.

Stevie slid her hand into the pocket and found the keys.

"I'll be back as soon as I can," she said.

"Good," said Max.

Stevie slid into the car, leaving the door open until she had the key in the ignition. She'd driven Carole's car before. She'd driven lots of cars before. She knew what she was doing . . . or did she?

The last time Stevie had driven a car, three people had nearly died. One was still recovering. And the horse . . . the horse. The horse was dying now. It would soon be over for him. It was Stevie's fault. She'd done it. She'd been driving. If only she'd managed to get the wheel a little more to the right—or had it been the left? If she'd hit him more in the center, would that have—

It didn't matter. She couldn't change it. She could only help him now.

She turned the key in the ignition. The engine came to life. *Judy, Judy, I have to get to Judy,* she told herself. *Fez needs her.*

She shifted the car into gear, realizing as she did it that she was back in the saddle. She was driving again.

FIFTEEN

Stevie found Judy at her truck in the driveway of Paget's Pride. Judy had overseen the birth of a healthy colt that was now taking his first meal of mare's milk. As soon as Stevie said, "Fez," Judy said, "You follow me. I'm less likely to get a ticket."

Stevie trailed the two red taillights along the country roads and across the highway. She was glad it was a clear night, because Judy was driving fast indeed, hovering just above the speed limit.

In much less time than Stevie had anticipated, the two of them pulled into the driveway at Pine Hollow. Judy paused to pick up her kit from the back of her truck and trailed Stevie into the barn.

They found the foursome still gathered around the horse. They had managed to get Fez to walk out into the paddock before he had fallen asleep under heavy sedation.

Emily, Callie, and the Foresters had joined the others. There wasn't anything to do but watch.

Ben told Judy what Fez's vital signs had been a half hour before. Judy checked his current vitals. The news was not good. His fever was up. His breathing was shallow and rapid.

"This isn't good," Judy said, folding her stethoscope. "This horse is very sick, and he's not going to get better."

Callie gasped. It didn't matter that this was the news that they'd been expecting. Hearing it, finally and absolutely, from Judy meant that she couldn't hope any longer.

"Is there anything you can do?" Callie's father asked. "I mean, if it's a matter of money . . ."

"No, it's not that," Judy said, standing up. "We've done everything, and then some." She looked at Ben. "His leg isn't healing as well as we'd hoped, and now he's developed an infection. In a way, it's his body's way of telling us that he isn't going to make it. He's feverish and in a great deal of pain. We can't allow him to suffer any longer.

"I have to make some phone calls," she went on. "There are technical and insurance issues with a horse this valuable. I'll be about half an hour. He's resting now with the sedative Max gave him, so at least he's not in pain."

Judy excused herself. Max followed her to his office, where she could use the phone, and Callie's father went along to help with the legal matters.

Mrs. Forester gave Callie a hug.

"I need to say good-bye to him," Callie said.

Ben, Phil, and Carole stepped away from the horse to let Callie get near him. She looked up at her friends and her mother. "By myself," she said.

"We'll be in the locker room," Carole told her. The group made its way there, leaving Callie alone with the horse she'd hardly had a chance to ride but that she'd loved so much.

Callie lowered herself onto the straw next to Fez and began patting his face soothingly. "I'm so sorry," she said. "This hasn't worked out at all the way we planned it. We were going to be great, you and I. We were going to ride in all the endurance competitions the East Coast had to offer us. We would have been a championship pairing, you know.

"Now look at us. I can't do anything right, and you can't do anything. You've worked so hard, suffering so much pain to try to heal. And now it's over. Your long journey is done; you're going home where broken legs, shattered hearts, and infections don't matter. You won't be in pain anymore. You won't have to try anymore. You won't even have to endure anymore. You can rest. Forever."

For a moment Fez seemed to understand her. His eyes fluttered open. He saw her, blinked, then closed his eyes again.

"Rest," she said again, repeating the word as if it were a mantra, trying to lead the horse to peace with her soft voice and her soothing touch.

Still whispering to Fez, still patting him softly, Callie leaned back against the smooth boards of the paddock fence. She closed her eyes, letting her tears stream down her cheeks. It was too much. Her hand became still on the horse's neck. She breathed with him. She slept.

Carole was the first to reach them. It didn't surprise her at all to find Callie asleep. Grief was exhausting. Carole put her finger to her lips, and everybody came quietly. Callie's father crouched next to Callie and took her hand. Her eyes opened.

"It's time," he said. "Do you want to leave?"

"No, I'll stay here," Callie told him. "Fez needs me now more than ever." She looked up at Judy. "He's ready," she said.

Carole and Stevie had seen horses put down

155

before. It was a horrible thing to have to do, but when it meant keeping the horse from continuing pain, it was the right thing.

Stevie reached over and took Carole's hand. She squeezed it. Carole squeezed back. She was awfully glad her friend was there with her. In fact, a lot of friends were there. Carole looked over at the Foresters. Scott had his arm around his mother's shoulder. Mrs. Forester was wiping a tear from her cheek, surely feeling as much pain for her daughter as she did sadness for the horse. Emily stood next to Max. They exchanged somber glances.

Ben stood alone. He watched silently. Carole knew he felt sorrow at seeing Fez put down. Anyone who loved horses hated to see that, hated to say good-bye to a friend, especially a friend he'd been looking after. But Fez had been more than a horse friend to Ben. Fez had been his project, his scholarship, his ticket to college.

"It's over," Judy said, standing up. "He's at peace."

SIXTEEN

Callie stood up then, accepting a hand from Judy. Callie's mother gave her her crutches.

"Excuse me," Callie said, then fled, as fast as her crutches would carry her, to the locker room.

Emily followed her, and so did the rest of her friends.

By the time Carole entered the locker room, Callie was crying uncontrollably.

"He was so brave!" she said, and it was true. Nobody knew that better than Carole and Ben. Carole would forever hold the image in her heart of the horse standing up that afternoon, just because they'd told him to do it, sick and pained as he was.

"Yes, he was," Carole said. "And now he doesn't have to be."

"It was all my fault," Stevie said, sitting down next to Callie on a bench.

"No, it wasn't," Ben said. "And it's time to stop blaming anyone. It was an accident. You couldn't help hitting the horse any more than Fez could help running out on the road in terror. There are no winners when a horse gets hit by a car. You three were lucky to escape alive. You've all learned things you might never have learned before."

"Like how to be crippled?" Callie asked bitterly, and then, ashamed, began to cry harder.

"Well, yes," Ben said. "And you've learned more about riding by not being able to do it well than you learned when it was easy for you, haven't you?"

Callie wiped the tears from her eyes. "You're looking for silver linings?"

"Is there something wrong with that?" Ben asked.

"Well, what was in it for Fez?" she challenged him.

Carole understood Callie's bitterness, and nobody there questioned her sharp remark about being crippled. What Carole knew that Callie didn't was that Fez's death held another meaning, another disappointment, another sadness for Ben. Her heart ached for him.

Mrs. Forester came in then. "I know this doesn't feel much like a party, but we've got an awful lot of food and sodas left at our house,

158

not to mention some guests who are waiting for us. I also suspect that there are a few of you who didn't feel you were judged fairly in the cannonball contest . . . ," she teased, trying to lighten the mood.

One by one they stood up. It seemed right to return to the party. Before they left Pine Hollow, they each stopped to say good-bye to Fez a final time.

Back at the Foresters', nobody could pretend to be in a partying mood. People began to drift away until just the Pine Hollow group and the Foresters remained. Scott had brought out a stereo and began playing soft, pleasant music. That helped a little. Callie's father returned to the grill and began turning out a new batch of ribs and chicken. That helped, too. Stevie and Phil got into the swimming pool, where she climbed up on his shoulders to dive. That also helped.

Emily sat down next to Callie.

"Listen, Emily, I'm sorry. That was uncalled for," Callie said.

"Don't worry about it," Emily said. "You're right, you know. There isn't much to be said for being different the way I always have been and the way you are now but probably won't always be. The advantage I have over you is that it's something I was born accepting."

"I still shouldn't have said that."

"No, you shouldn't have, but it's okay. I understand—probably better than the rest of them do. Anyway, I'm already seeing you make progress. You will heal. You'll be whole again soon."

"You think being normal means being whole?"

"It's one way of putting it," Emily said.

"Well, then you're home free because you're the most whole person I know."

"It isn't easy," said Emily.

Callie knew exactly what she meant.

Around them the party picked up. Ben convinced Carole to climb onto his shoulders in the pool, where she faced off with Stevie on Phil's shoulders. All four of them ended up in the water.

After that, Mrs. Forester organized the promised cannonball rematch. There was much discussion about the winner, but ultimately, when they all jumped into the pool at the same time, the winner was declared to be the group.

Finally, a quiet time. All the ribs and chicken had been eaten, the salads were gone, the chips and soda were fast disappearing. The group spread towels out on the lush grass and talked about things that mattered: friends and horses.

"I miss Lisa, you know," said Stevie. "I wish she were here."

"So much has happened," said Carole. "I mean since she left."

"Did someone say something about a Lisa?" Congressman Forester asked.

"She's our friend," Stevie explained. "She's in California for the summer."

"Well, she may be in California, but she's also on the phone," he said.

"Here?"

"Right here," he said, placing a cordless speaker phone in the middle of the group.

"Lisa?" Carole asked.

"It's me," Lisa said cheerfully on the other end of the line. "I was talking to Alex and he told me that you all were at the Foresters', and I thought, *I can't resist that, I've just got to call.* But I didn't know I'd be talking to you all at once."

"My dad's a gadget-meister," Callie said. "If somebody's invented something electronic, he can't resist it."

"Well, this is cool," Stevie said. "It's almost like having you here—"

"Except we don't have to share the chicken and ribs with her!" Scott joked.

"So what's new?" Carole asked.

"Not much since I talked to you guys, Carole and Stevie. But for the rest of you, I'm working like crazy—"

"Right," Stevie interrupted. "When she isn't living the glamorous life in the fast lane with the Young Turks of Hollywood."

"Give me a break. I hardly ever see them, except when they need their horses— Oops."

"What's oops?" Callie asked.

"Just a second," Lisa said. They waited, listening, hearing little except for a slight rumbling in the background and then the crash of a glass.

"What was that?" Stevie asked.

"Just a tremor," said Lisa.

"You mean like an earthquake?"

"Yeah, but it was a little thing. They happen all the time out here, only mostly we don't notice them."

"I heard a glass break," Emily said.

"I shouldn't have left it so close to the edge of the table," said Lisa. "Anyway, that doesn't matter. I want to know everything that's going on."

"Ben won the cannonball contest," Carole said.

"And I bet you two are having fun working together at Pine Hollow, right, Carole?" Lisa asked. "Max is so lucky having both of you."

Carole looked over at Ben, wondering if he felt that way at all. Nothing showed in his face, as usual.

"Ben, Carole told me everything you were doing for Fez. I'm sure you'll have him up and galloping in no time flat."

There was a silence that nobody wanted to fill right then. Carole and Stevie would tell Lisa what had happened when they spoke with her another time.

"Callie, are you there? Carole and Stevie told me you're working hard with PC. How's your ankle?"

"It's a lot better," Callie said.

"And by the way, Stevie, Alex tells me that you and he have a new car. I hope you're letting him drive it sometimes."

"I am," Stevie said.

Stevie and Carole exchanged looks. This phone call wasn't turning out the way they would have hoped. It felt as if Lisa, the usual voice of reason, was much further than three thousand miles away—in a land where the earth shook and nothing made sense.

"Hey, Lis', are you going to be home tomorrow?" Carole asked.

"I'll be home in the morning. Then in the afternoon, Skye and some of the other people from the cast are having a picnic on the beach."

"A beach picnic with the Hollywood brat pack?" Scott asked. "And you expect us to believe you're not having fun out there?"

"I didn't say I wasn't having fun," said Lisa. "But I did say I miss you guys. It's hard being so far away from my friends. So much is begun and so little is finished."

"I'll call you in the morning," Carole said.

First thing, thought Stevie. There was a lot Lisa had to catch up with.

"Okay, good night," Lisa told everyone.

"Good night," they chorused back. Stevie reached for the Off button on the speaker phone. That was definitely enough of that phone call.

"Do you think Lisa was calling from another planet?" Stevie asked later that night when she and Carole were alone at her house.

"It sure seemed that way, didn't it?" Carole said. "She's been gone, what, six weeks? And we've spoken with her and she's talked to us, but it's like we're in different worlds. And she doesn't have a clue."

"Neither do we," Stevie said. "Earthquakes—"

"Tremors."

"Whatever. Tremors, beach parties with Hollywood stars. What kind of life is that?" Stevie asked.

"A nice one," said Carole. "But we're her friends, and when she was talking, she kept putting her foot in it."

"There's no way she could have known about Fez," Stevie said.

"I know, I know. It's just that I'm used to Lisa being the one who always knows what's going on and always knows the sensible way to solve problems," Carole said. "It felt very strange to have her be so out of it."

"Maybe we're the ones who are out of it," Stevie said.

"What do you mean?" asked Carole.

"Remember what she said about so much begun, so little finished? That's what it is, you know. It's like we're in the middle of everything. All this stuff is up in the air and it's hard to live with things up in the air even if you know that eventually you'll have all the answers."

"And what if you don't like the answers?" Carole asked, wondering what answers would be in store for Ben.

"Like if Callie doesn't get better? Or if Lisa decides to stay in California?" Stevie suggested.

"Okay, those things, too," Carole said, trusting Stevie to know what else was on her mind.

"Then maybe we'll just have to pretend to

like them. I remember a time in our lives when we thought we could change everything that wasn't right, when we could right the wrongs and set the world straight."

"The world's a little bigger now," Carole agreed.

"So maybe we have to work a little harder."

Carole wondered if Stevie was pretending now, or if she was finally starting to believe that everything really would be all right again.

ABOUT THE AUTHOR

BONNIE BRYANT is the author of more than a hundred books about horses, including The Saddle Club series, Saddle Club Super Editions, and the Pony Tails series. She has also written novels and movie novelizations under her married name, B. B. Hiller.

Ms. Bryant began writing The Saddle Club in 1986. Although she had done some riding before that, she intensified her studies then and found herself learning right along with her characters Stevie, Carole, and Lisa. She claims that they are all much better riders than she is.

Ms. Bryant was born and raised in New York City. She still lives there, in Greenwich Village, with her two sons.

You'll always remember your first love.

Love Stories

Looking for signs he's ready to fall in love? Want the guy's point of view? Then you should check out the Love Stories series. Romantic stories that tell it like it is— why he doesn't call, how to ask him out, when to say good-bye.

Nothing's worse than having to spend every day with someone you hate... unless you have the thought of spending even one more day without him...

Who Do You LOVE?
Janet Quin-Harkin

SUPER EDITION
Daring.
Irresistible.
Totally necessary.
Meet Rob Barden.

It's Different for Guys
Stephanie Leighton

I wanted to be with Matt every minute of every day. Then I got my wish...

24/7
Amy S. Wilensky

The Love Stories series is available at a bookstore near you.